**W9-BGW-434**

> "We'll never be perfect. We can only do our best, take each day as it comes, and forgive ourselves for honest mistakes."

Inside Wade, a hard knot dissolved. Hearing the words in Adrienne's soft voice gave them power.

The power to heal. And the power to bring the two of them together.

Impulsively, Wade reached for her hands and rose, drawing her up. "I need you," he said, gathering her against him. With her hair flowing around him and her mouth inches from his, they were lost in a private, precious world.

"I need you, too," she whispered.

After that, there was no more place for words.

Dear Reader,

Readers often ask where writers get our ideas. Sometimes, we can't give a good answer, because we don't know. However, I can trace Adrienne and Wade's story to an article in my local newspaper.

A family attorney cited an influx of nurses from a hospital, eager to terminate the paternal rights of absentee biological fathers. The reason? At the hospital a woman had died, leaving a ten-year-old daughter who'd never known her father. This total stranger showed up, claimed his daughter and moved out of state, away from all her friends and other relatives. Because he'd never signed away his rights, he was able to do that. The horrified nurses hurried to the lawyer to protect their own children.

Adrienne, an obstetrician who works the night shift in Labor and Delivery, believes her late sister was abandoned by the father of her little boy, whom Adrienne plans to adopt. But Wade Hunter has a very different story, and he can prove it. Now who's going to raise little Reggie?

If you've read previous Safe Harbor Medical books, you'll recognize many of the characters. But if you're new to the series, don't worry. Each book stands alone.

Welcome to Adrienne and Wade's new world!

Best,

Jacqueline Diamond

# THE SURPRISE HOLIDAY DAD

—

## JACQUELINE DIAMOND

HARLEQUIN® AMERICAN ROMANCE®

If you purchased this book without a cover you should be aware that this book is stolen property. It was reported as "unsold and destroyed" to the publisher, and neither the author nor the publisher has received any payment for this "stripped book."

Recycling programs
for this product may
not exist in your area.

ISBN-13: 978-0-373-75504-2

THE SURPRISE HOLIDAY DAD

Copyright © 2014 by Jackie Hyman

All rights reserved. Except for use in any review, the reproduction or utilization of this work in whole or in part in any form by any electronic, mechanical or other means, now known or hereafter invented, including xerography, photocopying and recording, or in any information storage or retrieval system, is forbidden without the written permission of the publisher, Harlequin Enterprises Limited, 225 Duncan Mill Road, Don Mills, Ontario M3B 3K9, Canada.

This is a work of fiction. Names, characters, places and incidents are either the product of the author's imagination or are used fictitiously, and any resemblance to actual persons, living or dead, business establishments, events or locales is entirely coincidental.

This edition published by arrangement with Harlequin Books S.A.

For questions and comments about the quality of this book, please contact us at CustomerService@Harlequin.com.

® and TM are trademarks of Harlequin Enterprises Limited or its corporate affiliates. Trademarks indicated with ® are registered in the United States Patent and Trademark Office, the Canadian Trade Marks Office and in other countries.

**Printed in U.S.A.**

## ABOUT THE AUTHOR

Although Jacqueline Diamond's more than ninety published novels include romantic suspense, romantic comedy and Regency romances, medical stories are a particular favorite. Jackie's interest in medicine began with her father, who was the only doctor in the small town of Menard, Texas, before becoming a psychiatrist in Nashville, Tennessee. Jackie and her husband of thirty-five years live in Orange County, California, where she's active in Romance Writers of America. You can learn more about the Safe Harbor Medical series at www.jacquelinediamond.com and say hello to Jackie at her Facebook site, JacquelineDiamondAuthor.

### Books by Jacqueline Diamond

#### HARLEQUIN AMERICAN ROMANCE

# Chapter One

Wade Hunter trudged up the rickety stairs of the rent-by-the-week apartment hotel. As he climbed to his second-floor unit in the fading October daylight, he repeated the words that had kept him going in the months since the Northern California town of Pine Tree had laid off half its police force: "Today something will change my life for the better."

He didn't bother glancing at the handful of mail he'd pulled from his locked mailbox. That could wait until he sat down. His feet hurt from his part-time job providing private security for a cluster of warehouses, his cheek still smarted from the punch he'd taken at his second job as a bar bouncer and his heart ached from losing the close-knit group of fellow officers who'd been like a family.

*Quit feeling sorry for yourself. You'll turn this around.*

Inside, Wade tossed the envelopes and advertisements on a chipped end table. After hanging his jacket over the back of a chair, he kicked off his shoes and sank onto the creaky couch. With a sense of homecoming, he picked up his lovingly polished guitar and flexed his hands.

For a few indulgent moments, he fingered chords and hummed a country-and-western song. Not loudly, though. Downstairs neighbors had complained the last time he sang full-out.

What were they complaining about? It had been a reasonable hour, and he'd won prizes in karaoke contests.

Too tired to get up and stick a frozen dinner in the microwave, Wade reached for the mail. Most of it had been forwarded several times—there'd been an interim month when he stayed at a more expensive motel—but there was one address he'd kept current. And here it was, the envelope he'd been waiting for, from the California Bureau of Security and Investigative Services.

His breath catching in his throat, Wade opened it.

His muscles relaxed. It confirmed that he'd passed the exam to earn his private investigator's license. All he had to do was submit the licensing fee of $175.

*Ouch.* He'd been saving every penny he could, but that wasn't easy, especially with child-support payments. Still, this license might help Wade find a job with a detective agency. While he'd prefer a position at another police department, layoffs throughout California made that unlikely in the short term.

Becoming a P.I. wasn't what he'd dreamed of nearly a decade ago when he'd earned his degree in criminal justice. But if there was one thing Wade had learned in his thirty years, it was to focus on today and let the future take care of itself.

Invigorated by the sense of moving forward at last, he heated a beef dinner before scanning the other mail. Since he kept up with his bills and bank statements online, these were mostly ads. One long envelope, creased and marked with forwarding addresses, bore the logo of a law firm with a return address in the Southern California town of Safe Harbor.

Wade stiffened. The only people he'd stayed in touch with in his hometown were his father and, indirectly, a woman he'd rather not think about. Now here was a letter from Geoff Humphreys, attorney. According to the logo, the man specialized in family law.

No doubt this had something to do with Vicki Cavill. She'd driven Wade out of town by threatening to file false charges that could have derailed his law enforcement career. She'd also deprived him of the most precious thing in his life.

And, goaded by bad advice and his own immaturity, he'd let her.

No more running. Since the first of the year, she hadn't cashed his child-support checks. The woman was hopelessly disorganized. This wasn't the first time she'd gone for months before cashing a batch of checks, although it had never been this long.

Now she'd apparently hired a lawyer. Did she plan to shake him down for larger payments? If so, she'd have a fight on her hands.

He tore open the envelope.

"WHAT DO YOU mean he won't waive his parental rights?" Dr. Adrienne Cavill stared across the desk at Geoff Humphreys. "My sister barely knew him, and he abandoned his son as an infant. Vicki's will appointed me as Reggie's guardian. Why should what's-his-name have any rights?"

Hearing the shrillness in her voice, she stopped to take a deep breath. Working the overnight shift at Safe Harbor Medical Center's labor and delivery unit wreaked havoc on her body's sleep rhythms. And although the hospital's attorney had mentioned there might be complications when he'd referred her to Geoff, she hadn't anticipated any serious obstacles to adopting her nephew.

She wished now that she'd pushed harder to complete the adoption right after her sister's death in a single-car crash last New Year's Eve, but it had seemed little more than a formality. Also, between working long hours to pay off medical-school bills and providing a loving home for Reggie, Adrienne simply hadn't had the energy.

"Matters were not exactly as your sister represented them." With his receding hairline and calm manner, Geoff had a reassuringly paternal air. He was also the husband of a popular teacher at Reggie's elementary school and a father himself. "He's been sending checks to her at a post-office box. When I reached him by phone yesterday, he was wondering why they hadn't been cashed since the first of the year."

"He was helping support Vicki?" Adrienne hadn't paid much attention to her sister's messy finances, aside from the legal necessity of closing out Vicki's meager checking account and paying off her bills after her death. Suffering from bipolar disorder and drinking heavily, Vicki had spent every penny she earned as a housecleaner, and more. "She described him as a deadbeat."

"He emailed me copies of the canceled checks." Geoff gave a sympathetic sigh. "He also says that he sent gifts for his son. I presume she gave them to your nephew without revealing where they came from."

Adrienne could scarcely speak. "I had no idea." She rallied quickly. "But he's a total stranger to Reggie, and Vicki appointed me as guardian."

Geoff winced. Attorneys ought to have poker faces, Adrienne thought irritably, despite how much she'd appreciated his sympathetic glance a minute ago.

"I'm afraid that under California law, his rights trump yours," the lawyer said. "His name is on the birth certificate, and he informs me that he took a DNA test."

"And then skipped town," Adrienne replied bitterly. "Where was he when Vicki went off her medication and my mom was dying? I moved in with them for Reggie's sake. He could have used a father."

"According to Mr. Hunter, your sister threatened to accuse him of abuse and file a restraining order," Geoff said. "Since he was a police officer, that could have damaged or destroyed his career."

Vicki *had* been capable of unreasonable behavior. Despite a sweet and loving nature during her best periods, she'd been unstable, to put it mildly. That didn't excuse the man's neglect of his son. "Surely he's moved on. Married, with kids?"

"Not married, no kids," Geoff said. "I hate to mention it, but there's another issue."

*Oh, great.* "Which is?"

"As Reggie's father, he could claim control over the half interest in your house that his son inherited." The lawyer paused to let that bombshell sink in.

"He could *what?*" Adrienne wasn't sure why she bothered to reply, because she understood what she'd just heard. But it was unthinkable. "I'll see him in court."

Geoff raised a hand placatingly. "Naturally, a court will take into account what's best for the boy. You're an obstetrician with a steady income and a lifelong relationship with your nephew. And Mr. Hunter is, I understand, between jobs."

"Unemployed?" Typical of Vicki's boyfriends. "Naturally."

"However," the lawyer continued, "a court battle will be expensive and may not be in Reggie's best interest. In the worst-case scenario, Wade Hunter wins, insists you buy out his half of the house and takes his son away. And since you've become his enemy, he refuses to allow contact."

Tears of frustration burned behind Adrienne's eyelids. She'd weathered so much these past few years, standing strong for her sister while taking responsibility for Reggie. Did his so-called father have a clue how hard she'd worked to find trustworthy sitters, to maintain friendships that substituted for family and to nurture her vulnerable nephew?

"An antagonistic attitude isn't in your best interest or Reggie's," Geoff went on. "My recommendation is to reach an agreement with Mr. Hunter to share custody or to gain primary custody with generous visitation for him."

Adrienne felt an urge to pound on something, except that as a doctor, she didn't dare risk damaging her hands. Also, it would be childish. "What do you suggest I do next?"

Geoff smiled, clearly pleased at her decision to accept his advice. "He's driving down this weekend to stay with his father, who lives in town. He's eager to meet his little boy."

"If he thinks he can blow into Reggie's life and then out again…" Adrienne halted. Wasn't that exactly what she hoped Wade Hunter would do? "Fine. Reggie's sixth birthday party is Sunday but his real birthday isn't until next Tuesday. I suppose this man will expect to see his son on his birthday."

"I'll find out if he can meet with you and me before then to lay some ground rules. How about Monday?"

Since that was one of her days off, Adrienne nodded. "Early afternoon would be best."

"If it's any consolation, he seemed like a rational fellow on the phone."

Okay, so the man had paid support and sent a few presents. Still, it was hard to adjust her mental image when for so long she had pictured Reggie's father as a jerk.

And he *hadn't* been there for his son. Despite Vicki's threats, he could have tried harder.

As she left the office, Adrienne considered how to break the news to her nephew. At this age, Reggie spun fantasies about his dad being a superhero who would swoop in to rescue him if trouble threatened. All Wade Hunter had to do was show a little kindness, and he'd capture the boy's heart.

In reality it was Adrienne who'd swooped in to rescue Reggie. And she suspected that once this stranger tired of playing Daddy to a kid with real needs, she'd have to do it all over again.

Might as well wait until Monday to tell Reggie. She'd rather keep everything normal for him as long as possible.

WHEN WADE EXITED the freeway at Safe Harbor Boulevard, he inhaled the briny tang in the air with bittersweet nostalgia. This used to be his home. After six years away, he felt like a stranger.

Although he kept in touch with his father, Daryl, and they met for the occasional camping trip or for a weekend of watching NASCAR races, Wade rarely made the nine-hour drive to his hometown. His last visit had been years ago, and memories of a wrenching argument with his grandfather still stung. Now he figured he'd stay with Daryl while he secured his claim on his son and put out feelers for a job in the area.

Having worked at the Safe Harbor Police Department early in his career, Wade had applied there, but the department's tight budget meant there were no hiring plans. He'd received the same response at other nearby agencies.

But while he might not be able to provide little Reggie a home instantly, he intended to demand custody as soon as it became feasible. As for the kid's aunt, he appreciated that she'd stepped up to the plate in the past, but with a sister like Vicki, how reliable could she be, even if she was a doctor?

Wade steered his black sports coupe downhill from the freeway. At barely eight o'clock on Sunday morning, not much was stirring. He'd left Pine Tree late last night after working a final shift at the warehouse. Every paycheck counted.

To the south, he glimpsed an expanse of blue where the Pacific Ocean sprawled beyond the town's namesake harbor. Wade could also see the six-story medical center where Vicki had barred him from the maternity ward after Reggie's birth. Based on whatever she'd claimed about him, a guard had escorted him out, refusing to let him hold his son. Maybe he should have hired a lawyer and insisted on his rights, but the situation had caught him unprepared.

Anger and shame twisted inside him as he stopped for a red light. He'd do things differently now, but at twenty-four he'd been unsure of what it meant to be a father.

When he'd told his captain at the police department about Vicki's threat to file for a restraining order if he insisted on contact, the man had warned him to keep his distance. Pay the child support and be more careful who he hooked up with in future had been the gist of the captain's remarks. Wade's father had put it more succinctly: *Save yourself. Get the hell out of Dodge.*

Now everything was about to change. He had a son, and he refused to let anyone stand between them.

*Except that you have no idea how to be a father.* Daryl hadn't been much of a role model, acting more like a buddy than a parent. And in Pine Tree most of Wade's socializing had been with other bachelors.

Well, he intended to learn. There were books and the internet and, he hoped, some long-dormant instincts.

A few blocks farther, he turned into an apartment complex and parked in a visitor's spot. Carrying his laptop, his guitar and a duffel bag containing essential gear, he followed a path to the manager's unit.

Carefully, Wade twisted the knob. His father, who got free rent by handling caretaker duties in addition to his job as a mechanic, had promised to leave his place unlocked rather than be awakened this early.

The instant the door opened, the smell of beer hit him. He stopped, uneasy. His father had a tendency to go on occasional drinking binges, punctuated by periods of sobriety. Daryl always claimed he could control his drinking, and despite serious doubts about that, Wade realized he had no power to run his father's life.

He was reaching for the light switch when he heard a snore. As his eyes adjusted to the dimness, Wade made out his father sprawled on the couch, sitting with his head thrown back as if he'd fallen asleep while watching TV. A couple beer cans littered the coffee table, but the TV was off. It must have a sleep setting.

Morning light, faint as it was, proved unkind to Daryl Hunter. Even at this angle, Wade could see the pallor of his father's skin, the red veins in his nose and the thinning hair. Some of that might merely be signs of age, but— quick mental calculation—his dad was only fifty-two. At roughly the same age, the police chief in Pine Tree looked healthy and fit. Or had until he'd gained a few worry lines over the layoffs.

Stepping softly to avoid disturbing his father, Wade headed into the bedroom. The smell of unwashed sheets gave him pause. He hoped this was a weekend spree rather than an indication that his father's condition was deteriorating.

Daryl had left his career as an Orange County deputy sheriff years ago, supposedly because he hated the shift schedule, although later Wade had wondered if alcohol had been a factor. Then he'd worked for a while at Grandpa Bruce's detective agency, Fact Hunter Investigations, but Daryl and Grandpa had butted heads. Not surprising considering Bruce's rigid nature, which was one reason Wade wouldn't consider applying there now.

After depositing his cases on the carpet, he went out to his car and brought in his large bag and bedroll. In the living room, Daryl had shifted position and was now snoring full force.

Wade unrolled the sleeping bag on top of the bed and

took off his shoes. As he lay waiting for sleep, he conceded that two things had become obvious.

He should forget about trying to find a job through his father's contacts; if Daryl was drinking heavily, a recommendation from him was more likely to work against Wade than for him. Also, the sooner he found a job and his own apartment, the better.

BY NOON THE rackety-rackety sound of skate wheels outside put an end to Wade's sleep. Irritated, he prowled out of the bedroom and said a quick hello to his father, who nodded from the small kitchen table. Daryl had poured himself a bowl of cereal and a glass of orange juice.

"Sorry, no welcome party." His father gave him a shaky smile. "Extra key's on the hook there. Bottom left." He indicated a Peg-Board.

"Thanks." Wade took it and went to shower, using the towels he'd brought. Then he stripped the bed, collected dirty towels and a box of detergent and went next door to the complex's laundry room to start a load. Since he'd taken over this chore at thirteen following his parents' divorce, the process felt familiar.

Back at the unit, Daryl had gone out, leaving a note that he was showing an apartment to a potential renter. Wade poured some cereal and checked his email while he ate. The attorney had confirmed a meeting at his office tomorrow with Dr. Cavill. The messages said she was willing to grant a supervised visit with Reggie on Tuesday, the boy's birthday.

A supervised visit? The hell with that. Wade didn't appreciate having this lady boss him around, and he didn't plan to wait two days to see his son, either. Nervous energy surged through him. *My boy.* Although he didn't yet have a sense of Reggie's personality—how could he?—he felt a connection deep in his gut, a longing that he'd strained for years to deny. He was angry, too, at the woman who'd put him in this position and at himself for yielding.

How would the little boy react to meeting his dad after all these years? While it might be awkward, he hoped Vicki's sister had had the decency to prepare her nephew for this major life change.

He recalled meeting Adrienne only once. She was blond like Vicki and had barely acknowledged the introduction, muttering an excuse about her busy schedule before brushing past him and out of the house. She'd been in her last year of medical school, as he recalled.

The lawyer had claimed that Adrienne was unaware that her sister had tried to wreck his career and that he'd made regular child-support payments. Maybe, maybe not.

By two-thirty the laundry was done. Daryl had returned and gone out again to repair a tenant's sink, so Wade locked the door and went to his car. From the trunk, he withdrew the toy police-station set he'd bought for his son's birthday. Although it was a few days early, a gift might help to smooth their meeting.

Relying on memory, he navigated across town toward the Cavill home. Passing his old hangouts—Krazy Kids Pizza, where he'd celebrated childhood birthdays, the Corner Tavern, where he and his fellow officers used to play pool, even the Bull's Eye Shooting Range—reminded him that he'd accepted his exile too easily. He'd missed this place.

As Wade left the commercial area and rolled through quiet residential streets, it hit him once again that he was about to meet the most important person in his life. Vicki had, grudgingly, sent a few photographs after Wade threatened to withhold payments. The last one, which he carried in his wallet, showed a boy of about four, blond, with a couple teeth missing. Cute little guy.

Now the kid was turning six. At that age, Wade had still

had his mother, along with a dad who wore a uniform and carried a badge. Although Wade had sensed undercurrents of tension, he'd trusted his parents to take care of him.

What about Reggie? The kid must have been stunned and overwhelmed when his mom died. Wade was sixteen when he'd lost his own mother in a small-plane crash three years after she and his father divorced. Although she'd moved away and they rarely saw each other, he'd been devastated.

If only he'd known about Vicki's death, he'd have rushed down here. Well, he'd do his best to compensate for that now.

After a couple wrong turns, he found the cul-de-sac. Picking the right house proved harder than expected. There were several two-story Craftsman structures with wide front porches, none of which matched his memory of fading beige paint and a patchy lawn edged by boxy hedges.

It had to be the one on the left, almost to the end. Wade recognized that row of sash windows on the second floor with a tiny attic window above. The house had been repainted cream with blue trim and the hedges replaced by blooming bird-of-paradise plants interspersed with hibiscus bushes, fronted by a mixture of miniature roses and colorful annual flowers. The doctor took good care of her property.

From the porch roof hung a bunting banner, each one of its green triangles displaying a picture of a teddy bear. A cluster of green and white balloons fluttered from one of the supports.

As he parked, he saw a bouncy little girl and her parents stroll toward the front door. There was something familiar about the mother, who had short stick-straight hair and the low-hipped stride of a cop accustomed to wearing a duty belt. When she glanced toward him, Wade recognized her as Patty Hartman, one of his fellow rookie officers from his stint at the local P.D. She carried a wrapped present.

After making startled eye contact with Wade, Patty waved. He returned the gesture.

Several more children scampered up the walkway with parents in their wake. They, too, brought gifts.

Reggie's birthday might not be until Tuesday, but the aunt had obviously scheduled his party for today. And Wade wasn't invited.

Well, he'd just invited himself.

## Chapter Two

With Anne Murray singing "Teddy Bears' Picnic" from a boom box on the patio, Adrienne hurried along the outdoor tables, distributing containers of Play-Doh along with teddy-bear molds.

"I should have done this earlier," she fretted to Harper Anthony, whose seven-year-old daughter, Mia, was romping with Reggie in the large backyard. "I'm usually better organized."

"I'd say you're remarkably well organized." That was a high compliment coming from Harper's fiancé, Peter Gladstone, a gifted teacher and sports coach. He indicated the refreshment table with a tray of cut-up vegetables, the teddy bear–themed yo-yos awaiting the guests and the decorated party hats, plates and gift bags. "This is impressive."

"That's due as much to my friends as to me," Adrienne protested. Through the kitchen window, she could hear newlyweds Stacy and Cole Rattigan bustling about fixing sandwiches.

Harper and Stacy had been close friends with Adrienne's younger sister since junior high. Both nurses, they'd done their best to steer Vicki into treatment for her bipolar disorder and her drinking, and since her death had pitched in to babysit Reggie when his regular sitter wasn't available. They'd also become Adrienne's allies and mutual support system.

Harper, who'd volunteered to take pictures today, snapped the two children as they chased a butterfly. "You seem on edge. Is everything okay?"

"I've noticed that, too," said Stacy, bringing a bowl of teddy-bear graham crackers from the kitchen. "What's going on?"

With guests due to arrive any minute, Adrienne hesitated to spill the news she'd kept to herself all week. But it had to come out sometime. "It's about the adoption. Reggie's birth father is contesting it."

"What?" Harper stared at her in dismay. "That lowlife?"

Stacy smacked the bowl onto the table. "Where does he get the nerve?"

"And if he takes my little boy away, I don't know what I'll…" Adrienne broke off.

"He can't!" Stacy protested.

"Unthinkable," Harper added. "If you need money for a lawyer, we'll help."

"So will we."

"Thank you." Adrienne struggled to regain her composure. "I already have an attorney. Unfortunately, he believes Wade has a case."

"What kind of case?" Harper's eyes narrowed.

"It turns out Vicki didn't tell the whole story." Adrienne explained about the checks and gifts.

"Sending money isn't the same as being a father." Stacy's hand dropped to her abdomen, visibly enlarged with triplets due in four months. "I don't know how I'd get through this pregnancy without Cole."

"A real dad does whatever it takes to protect his kids," Harper said. "Look how far Peter was willing to go to have children."

A widow with a young daughter, she'd donated eggs so that Peter—himself widowed—could have a child by a surrogate. Unexpectedly, the two had fallen in love and were now due to be parents next June. They'd been overjoyed to learn that the surrogate was carrying twin boys.

Adrienne glanced toward the interior of the house, expecting to hear the bell, which she'd turned on high for today. No one had arrived yet, though, giving her a few more minutes. "I haven't even told Reggie his father might be here next week."

"When are you planning to break the news?" asked Peter.

"As soon as Wade actually shows up. He's driving down from Northern California." Adrienne wanted Reggie to enjoy his party without stewing about his father.

"Good plan," Stacy said. "Considering he's been the invisible man until now."

Harper folded her arms. "Maybe he'll conveniently get lost on the way."

That would be a welcome break, Adrienne thought. "Just as long as he signs that legal waiver."

The bell jangled. "The happy hordes descend," Stacy murmured.

Through the window, Cole waved. "I'll get it." Wearing a checkered apron and a dab of chocolate icing on his cheek, he didn't look like a world-famous men's fertility expert.

"Thanks," Adrienne called.

She might as well relax and enjoy the party. No sense dwelling on what next week would bring.

WADE SUPPOSED HE shouldn't be surprised to find a man playing host at the front door. Yet the lawyer hadn't mentioned that Adrienne had a husband or fiancé.

Patty's family had already gone inside, followed by several other groups. The mild-looking fellow kept the door open for Wade, announcing, "Hi. I'm Cole."

"Wade Hunter." No sign of recognition crossed the man's face as they shook hands.

Cole's forehead wrinkled. "You were, uh, invited, right?"

"Do lots of little boys have stray men crashing their parties with gifts?" Wade wasn't sure why he felt cranky toward this guy, except that he'd stolen the father's place today.

"Sorry. It's just that we haven't met." Despite the apologetic tone, Cole remained blocking the entrance.

"You know all Dr. Cavill's friends?"

"Not exactly," the man conceded. "My wife probably does. Stacy. She's a surgical nurse at the hospital. Do you know her?"

*Way to act like an idiot, Wade.* "Afraid not." He decided to cut to the point. "I'm Reggie's father."

Still looking puzzled, Cole moved aside. "I didn't realize… Come on in. The party's in back."

The scents of chocolate and cinnamon reached Wade the instant he stepped into the foyer. Quite a charming change from his father's place, as were the bouncy music and cheerful voices drifting from the depths of the house. His mood lifting, he followed Cole.

Glancing into the living and dining rooms that opened off the hall, he saw comfortable, well-maintained furniture, with bouquets of flowers that he guessed came from the yard. Everything appeared tidy and fresh.

With a twist of longing, Wade recalled the house where he'd lived before his mother left. More modest than this one but just as inviting, it had smelled of lemon oil and baking. He'd hurried in after school each day, eager to eat his snack and spill the day's events to Mom.

Not that last year, though. Once he entered adolescence, Wade recalled with embarrassment, he'd become surly and quick to rush off with his friends. No wonder his mother hadn't believed he'd needed her any longer.

Now, passing the staircase, he entered the family room. Judging by the view through the bay window, most of the action was on the patio. "I'd better go check on the food," Cole said. "Nice to meet you."

"My pleasure." Wade stayed where he was, not quite ready to plunge into the mix of people outside.

He was alone in the den except for two school-age girls who stood near the window. They seemed to be debating whether to take their stuffed animals outside and risk getting them dirty. Boys would never argue over something like that, Wade thought in amusement.

"Mischief wants to run around," said the shorter of the pair, a little charmer with elfin features. "He's restless."

"He should follow Roar's example." Her taller companion, a graceful African-American girl, cradled her lion. "He'd rather watch the others and write about them later."

"I guess that's okay." The first girl clutched her well-worn bear. "Mischief, we can play later, okay?"

The girls set their little pals in the bay window facing the yard and darted out through the kitchen. Following, Wade spotted Cole hovering near the oven.

"I'd forgotten that boys this age still have girls as friends," Wade remarked.

"Berry and Kimmie are stepsisters," Cole said, as if answering an unasked question. "Took them a while to warm up to each other, but now they're best pals." A timer rang. "Excuse me. That's the gluten-free cupcakes."

"Gluten-free cupcakes?"

"Some of the kids and parents have allergies."

Wade wondered how people kept track of such things. He'd have bought a cake at the store and been done with it.

Moving through the sunny kitchen, he stopped by an open slider window to take in the scene. A handful of adults gathered on the patio while children galloped on the grass and walkways. Among the three or four little boys, he couldn't tell which was Reggie.

He ought to recognize his own son. Thanks to Vicki, he couldn't.

Behind them a vegetable garden still flourished in October. Wade identified squash, peppers and a stubborn tomato plant. Nice touch. His mom used to raise herbs and vegetables, too.

Returning his attention to the patio, he noted a gift table. *Should have wrapped this thing,* he reflected. At least he'd attached a card.

After setting the box on the pile, he tried to pick out Reggie's aunt among her guests. Definitely the pretty blonde woman with her hair pulled back, although those coveralls didn't fit his image of a starchy professional. Why was she hiding in such a shapeless garment? It failed to disguise her attractive figure, however, just as the no-frills hairstyle didn't detract—much—from her lively face, intelligent light green eyes and full mouth.

Wade registered the instant she recognized him. Disbelief flashed across her face, then disapproval, yielding at last to a painful attempt at a smile. Well, if she'd invited him, she wouldn't have received such a shock.

As she started in his direction, a tall woman with long brown hair followed her gaze, then said something and indicated the children. Adrienne nodded, and her friend—corralling a couple other parents, including Patty—began distributing yo-yos in the yard.

With the others occupied, Adrienne approached Wade, her expression wary. "I wasn't expecting you today." Her warm, low voice stated that as a fact, not a challenge.

Wade decided to try a diplomatic approach. As a police officer, he'd learned that a courteous tone often defused potential violence, not that he expected anyone to start throwing punches around here. "You've put together a great party. I didn't mean to crash, but I was in the neighborhood."

She raised an eyebrow.

"On purpose," he admitted. "I was impatient to meet my son. Only I didn't expect all these people."

Adrienne swallowed. "I thought it would be better for you to meet him next week, just the three of us."

"I'd prefer just the two of us." Seeing her chin come up defiantly, he changed the subject. "How's he taking the news?"

"What news?"

"About me." That ought to be obvious, he thought.

She averted her gaze. "I haven't told him yet."

Anger boiled up, hot and fast. She hadn't bothered to prepare his son, leaving Wade to break the news himself. "Did you think about his feelings?"

"That's all I thought about!" She glanced around, but no one stood near enough to overhear her sharp tone.

"Could have fooled me."

"You might consider my perspective." Tension bristled in her voice. "What if you didn't show up? I've spent the past year helping my nephew deal with losing his mom. That's all he needs, to get excited about his daddy and then be left with nothing."

"I wouldn't do that," he said tightly.

"You accused me of ignoring Reggie's feelings," she responded. "That's not fair."

Much as he hated to admit it, she had a point. "Perhaps."

She folded her arms. "Look, Mr. Hunter…"

"Wade."

"Wade. Until a few days ago, I believed you were a deadbeat who dumped my sister and abandoned my nephew." Her commanding expression warned him not to speak until she finished. "I understand now that wasn't the case. But I love Reggie more than anything. I will make whatever sacrifices are necessary to give him a stable, loving home."

"So will I." He meant that, even though he wasn't sure how to accomplish it. Nevertheless, he grasped quite clearly what lay ahead when Reggie hit adolescence. This aunt might be strong—no doubt a lot stronger than her sister—but that didn't mean she could rein in a young man with roaring hormones and a family tendency to screw up. "He needs a dad. I wish I'd been involved all along, but I'm here now."

Her shoulders tightened. "We can't resolve this today."

"Agreed. Well?"

"Well, what?"

"I'd like to meet him," he said with strained patience.

Adrienne's lips formed a thin line before she answered. "Let's wait for the right moment, okay?" she asked. "So we can do this discreetly, without disrupting the party."

Since he disliked creating a scene, Wade had no problem agreeing. "That suits me." In the yard, the children had spread out to experiment with their yo-yos. "Which one is he?"

Adrienne looked astonished at the question and then responded wryly, "The dirt magnet."

Wade laughed. No question, that was the blond boy vying with a couple girls to spin his yo-yo the farthest. The knees of his jeans were smeared with something brown and crusted, while a large leaf stuck to his hair.

One of the parents in the yard plucked off the leaf and said something about it. Reggie's mouth formed the word "Yeah?" and he took the leaf, examining its shape.

"That's Peter Gladstone, my friend Harper's fiancé," Adrienne said. "He was Reggie's coach at sports camp last summer. He teaches biology and physical education."

"I went to sports camp when I was a kid." The implication that other men had filled the role of father figure troubled Wade. Still, that was better than no father figures at all. "I suppose it's good for Reggie to have his coach as a friend."

"It is." Adrienne edged away. "I should be out there running the party."

"Don't let me stop you."

"They're going overboard with the yo-yos." She waved at a boy swinging his wildly. "Hey! Cut it out!"

Peter moved in and calmed the child. Otherwise, Wade would have been tempted to intervene and possibly assign a dozen push-ups to take the edge off the kid's exuberance.

"It's time for the teddy-bear modeling session." Facing the youngsters, Adrienne cupped her hands over her mouth. "Play-Doh, everybody!"

As the parents shepherded the children toward the tables, Patty spotted Wade. "Hey, Reggie!" she announced in a voice loud enough to halt a fleeing perp a block away. "Look, your dad's here!"

Beside Wade, Adrienne stiffened. So much for waiting for the right moment, he thought, and prepared to meet the son he'd missed for all these years.

A BEAM OF sunlight lit Reggie's face as the little guy registered what Patty had said. Adrienne's chest squeezed. How would he react? Even if things went well today, she dreaded to think how devastated he'd be if, eventually, Wade let him down.

The man had a muscular, self-contained presence that under other circumstances she'd have found attractive. Not today. He'd come where he wasn't invited and had the nerve to criticize her. Had he waited until Reggie's actual birthday, she'd have laid the groundwork.

Well, there was no going back after Patty's blunt declaration. Her friend—who'd married hospital embryologist Alec Denny and become stepmother to seven-year-old Fiona—had a kind heart but rough edges.

Reggie trotted toward them and then stopped in confusion. He blinked at Wade as if the man had stepped out of a TV set. "Is he really my dad?" he asked Adrienne.

"Yes." How was she going to handle this? Wade's untimely arrival had forced her hand. "It's…a birthday surprise." *Boy, does that sound lame.*

"Hi, Reggie," the man said. "Happy birthday."

"Uh, hi." The little boy reached out and patted his father's arm gingerly, as if Wade were a crouching lion, both fascinating and scary.

"Hugs!" Patty called, cheering them on. It occurred to Adrienne that since she hadn't told her friend about Wade in advance, Patty must have known him in her former job at the police department.

A smile illuminated Wade's rugged face. Bending down, he closed his arms around his son. After a moment's uncertainty, Reggie's arms encircled his neck. On the sidelines, Harper snapped a picture of the tableau.

"How about going inside so we can talk in private?" Wade said.

Reggie looked up uncertainly. "Is that okay, Aunt Addie?"

Refusing might bring on an awkward dispute. "Just for a minute. I'll make sure you don't miss anything important out here."

With a deep breath, the boy she loved with every fiber of her being took the big man's hand and went indoors with him. Reg was so small, so powerless. *Don't let him become a pawn in this guy's ego trip.*

While Peter steered everyone's attention to a game, Harper joined Adrienne on the patio. "Is he being a complete jerk?"

She wasn't sure how to respond. The man was tearing her world apart, and she hated him for it. But she'd seen his tenderness and the glint of moisture in his gray eyes as he'd embraced his son.

"Not a complete jerk," she responded at last.

"Let us know what we can do," Harper said loyally.

"I will." Adrienne thanked heaven for her friends.

SITTING ON A couch in the den to be near Reggie's height, Wade searched for the right way to begin. He settled on, "Did your aunt tell you anything about me?"

The little guy shook his head.

Waded wished they could skip this difficult conversation and cut to the fun part, where he taught his son to surf or play Frisbee or trounce an opponent at Ping-Pong. The guy stuff, instead of all these emotions.

It struck him, though, that this conversation might stand out forever in his son's memory—the key moment when Reggie found out the truth about his dad. Turning points like this stayed with a person. One holiday when Wade served charity meals to the homeless, he'd sat down later with an eighty-year-old man who'd reminisced about the day his father came home from the war, describing with heartfelt clarity the details of an event seventy years in the past.

*Let's start with the important part.* "I love you," Wade said. "I've always loved you."

"Mom told me you didn't care." The boy's tongue traced a gap in his teeth where a new one was growing. "That you left us."

"She forced me to leave." Much as he disliked maligning the dead, Vicki didn't deserve to get off easy.

Reggie considered this. "How?"

"Your mom had security guards throw me out of the hospital. She told them I was violent, but I never did anything like that." Wade's anger rose at the memory. "She lied about me and tried—well, threatened—to have me arrested. I'm a police officer. I'd have been fired from the police department."

Reggie folded his hands in front of him. "Mom acted kind of crazy sometimes."

"I'm sorry you had to see that," Wade said. "And I'm sorry I wasn't here to protect you. I should have been."

"Aunt Addie keeps me safe."

A spurt of gratitude replaced his annoyance at the doctor, temporarily anyway. "I'm glad she's taken care of you. Now I'm here to do that."

"Why?" Reggie asked.

"Because I love you."

"I mean, why'd you come back now?"

A reasonable question. "I just found out your mother died. I've been living up in Northern California." Wade brushed his palm across his son's cheek. "I drove to Safe Harbor as soon as I could."

"How long will you stay?"

Suggesting that he might remove the boy from his home would be a bad idea, Wade surmised. "Forever, if I can find a job." Silence descended. After waiting a bit, he said, "Any more questions?"

"No." Although the boy would probably think of plenty later—this was a heavy conversation for a young kid, Wade acknowledged. Reggie glanced past him out the window. "Did you bring that police-station set?"

Swiveling, Wade saw his gift sitting atop the others. "Sure did."

"Can we play with it?"

*He's a normal kid. Toys first.* Wade chuckled. "I'd like that. But everybody else brought presents, too. It might hurt their feelings if you play with mine and not theirs."

"All right." Reggie wiggled impatiently. Standing in one place for more than a few seconds was obviously a foreign concept at this stage of his development. "Can I go outside?"

"You bet."

The boy stepped forward and then halted. "What should I call you?"

Longing seized Wade. *Go for what you want.* "Daddy sounds good to me."

The child appeared to be weighing the matter seriously. "Now that I'm six, I'd rather call you Dad."

"Done." Wade held up his hand. To his satisfaction, his little boy ran over and fist-bumped him before scooting out.

That had gone well, or so Wade assumed. If only he knew more about kids and their thought processes.

*Well, I'll learn.*

REG TROTTED OUT, eager to join his friends. Adrienne couldn't tell much from his expression. Through the window, he'd appeared to do more listening than usual, while his father appeared to have treated the boy with respect.

She still wished the man would leave them alone.

Wade rejoined her on the patio. "He says you took care of him when his mom…didn't. Thank you for that."

"He seems in good spirits." A bit grudgingly, Adrienne added, "Thank *you* for handling that tactfully."

"Did that hurt?"

"Did what hurt?"

"Thanking me." His playful tone took the edge off his words. At close range, she noted that his eyes were silver-gray, like Reggie's. Adrienne had never seen anyone else with that exact shade.

"Yes," she answered honestly. No matter how civil this man was, nothing changed the fact that he might try to take her child away. "We're meeting tomorrow at the lawyer's, right?"

Wade's head tilted in accord. "I'm surprised a doctor like you is free on a weekday."

"I work an overnight shift in Labor and Delivery, plus some evening office hours."

His forehead furrowed. "Who stays with Reggie?"

"He has a regular sitter—she's licensed." Adrienne resented being interrogated. Still, she supposed the question was warranted. "He sleeps at her house with her family. Occasionally on weekends, if she has other commitments, he stays with Harper or Stacy."

"That can't be easy for him." Wade shifted position, showing signs of restlessness. *Just like his son.*

"I sleep while he's in school, and I'm usually here when he gets home." *Enough about that. I don't have to defend myself.* "You're a police officer. Surely you've worked overnights."

"Well, yes."

"Then you should understand that we adapt as best we can. Especially parents."

He nodded slowly. "I'm sure I'll find out."

The implication chilled her. "He lives here. With me."

"For now," Wade said coolly. "Well, I think I'll take off. Don't want to interrupt the party any more than necessary." He went over to Reggie, who was eagerly pressing his mold over a mound of soft Play-Doh, and rested a hand on the boy's shoulder. "Hey, kid, I'm leaving, but I'll see you Tuesday on your actual birthday."

"And we'll play with the police set?" The little boy gazed up at him. "Shoot some bad guys?"

"Shoot some pretend bad guys." Wade's grin transformed him into the young, open-faced man he'd been when Adrienne had met him all those years ago, she recalled abruptly. If she wasn't careful, she might start to like him.

Her earlier image of him as a crouching lion came to mind. No matter how appealing he seemed, there was no telling if or when he might pounce.

# *Chapter Three*

For Wade, social events, unless they involved watching football games, quickly wore thin. The aversion dated from his childhood, when family gatherings had usually degenerated into arguments involving either Mom vs. Dad or Daryl vs. Grandpa Bruce.

This one seemed pleasant, though. Wade was glad he'd had a chance to meet, or at least observe, some of the other parents. They obviously played a major role in Reggie's life.

When he'd speculated about seeking employment out of town and taking Reggie with him, he hadn't considered the other people in his son's life. Moreover, everything about Reggie, from his healthy appearance to his trusting nature, showed Adrienne's loving care. Wade had to admit that the aunt was doing a fine job. Still, if it came to a choice between claiming his son and losing him again, Wade knew which choice he'd make.

He cut through the kitchen. "Leaving already?" Peter, the teacher and coach, was arranging candles on a bear-shaped chocolate cake while a couple other people worked at the counter. "I don't blame you. If you aren't used to being around kids, the noise level can be grating."

"Yeah, it's new to me." Wade searched for a polite question and hit on "Which one's yours?"

"Mia, the little girl with short brown hair and a snub nose, is about to become my stepdaughter," the man said.

"Harper and I are getting married the day after Thanksgiving. Adrienne's been kind enough to let us have the ceremony here."

"Generous of her." Seemed like a lot of work, but women enjoyed planning weddings. And birthday parties, and Christmas celebrations, Wade thought wistfully, remembering his mother. Once again his heart went out to his son. Vicki might have been—*had* been—a messed-up individual, but she'd still been Reg's mom.

After a polite farewell, Wade turned to go. Patty popped into his path holding a tray of sandwiches. "Hungry?" she asked. "There's peanut butter, tuna fish and grilled cheese with tomatoes. It tastes good even though it's healthy."

His stomach growled as his hand hovered over the tray.

"Take one of each. They're small." She shook back her fine, straight hair. "Hey, so I guess there's a story about why you left town. I never bought that stuff about wanting a change of scenery."

"Yes. A *long* story." He bit into the first sandwich. The cheese nearly melted in his mouth.

Patty set the tray down nearby. "While you're eating, here's my pitch. We could use another hand at the agency and you'd fit right in. Mike Aaron bought it, you know."

Wade had no idea what she was talking about, although he did recall Mike Aaron as a detective at the P.D. "Which agency?"

"Fact Hunter." Patty regarded him curiously. "You knew your grandfather sold it, right?"

"I had no idea." Wade hadn't spoken with his grandfather since their bitter quarrel several years ago. Although Bruce Hunter had been furious that Wade had refused to quit his job in Pine Tree and join the investigations agency, the old man hadn't mentioned selling it.

Maybe he'd been irate because he'd hoped his grandson's joining him would allow him to keep it afloat. No doubt Bruce had had too much pride to admit he couldn't keep running the place by himself in his seventies. Well, he should have said so. Might not have changed anything, but Wade, who'd resented what he'd seen as an attempt to control him, might have responded more gently.

"You and your grandpa don't talk much, eh?" Patty said. "Well, Mike bought the agency a couple years ago with his brother, Lock."

"Lock? Don't think I've met him." Despite Wade's urge to leave, those sandwiches were tasty. Judging by the number of trays still on the counter, there were plenty for this crowd.

"Short for Sherlock, which is perfect for a detective, huh? He was a sheriff's deputy in Arizona," she explained. "Yeah, well, then I came on board when I got married. Being a stepmom's important, and I'd had it with those night shifts—you understand."

Mouth full, Wade nodded.

"Mike's brought in some new clients and we're stretched thin," she went on. "Fraudulent insurance claims, attorneys needing evidence, companies doing background checks on new hires. Dull stuff, but it pays the bills. You could work on your P.I. license under his supervision."

"Just got it," Wade said.

"Perfect!" Scrounging in her pocket, Patty withdrew a business card. "There's the office number. I'll tell Mike to expect your call."

"Pushy little thing, aren't you?" he teased, although she was only a few inches shorter than him.

"Always."

Wade took the card. Fact Hunter Investigations. Who'd have imagined he'd ever consider working there? "Maybe I will."

"Good seeing you." She reclaimed the tray. "Reggie's a cute little dude."

"I think so, too."

As he ducked out, it occurred to Wade that his father hadn't bothered to mention the sale of the agency. Surely he'd heard about it, if only afterward.

It would be a stroke of luck finding a position in Safe Harbor. Being a father was a complicated business, Wade could see. Living near Reg's friends and aunt would mean not having to tear his son away from familiar surroundings. They'd be able to get acquainted gradually, building a relationship step-by-step.

Things looked promising. A little too promising. In Wade's experience, the minute you got comfortable, matters exploded in your face.

All the same, he might give Mike Aaron a call.

"You didn't have a clue he was coming?" Harper asked as she and Adrienne tossed out the last dropped teddy-bear grahams and torn pieces of party hat.

The other parents had helped clean up, too, so there wasn't much left to do. With Stacy tiring easily due to her pregnancy, Adrienne had sent her and Cole home.

Mia and Reggie had carted his gifts to his room. The pair, who acted more like brother and sister than friends, was playing happily with all those new toys, judging by the squeals and giggles drifting from the upstairs window.

"We're meeting with the attorney tomorrow to set some ground rules." Since Adrienne didn't care to discuss Wade further, even with a close friend, she changed the subject. "You're sure you want to plan the wedding outdoors? The weather can be tricky in late November." While Southern California enjoyed mild winters, that didn't preclude rain.

Concerned about the cost of a wedding, Harper and Peter had discussed asking his parents, who lived inland, to hold it at their house. But their place was fairly small, so Adrienne had offered up hers. She enjoyed seeing her home full of friends.

"I prefer a garden setting, and if we keep everything outside, there's less cleanup." Since it was the second wedding for both bride and groom, they were taking an informal approach. The guest list was short, and the only members of the wedding party would be Peter's father as best man and Mia as flower girl. Instead of a white gown, Harper had selected a knee-length dress in autumnal shades: golden-yellow, tawny-brown and red-orange.

"Of course, we can move inside if necessary," Adrienne mused.

"You're incredibly thoughtful." Harper dropped a lump of hardening Play-Doh into the trash bag. "Some people prefer to reserve Black Friday for their Christmas shopping." They'd scheduled the wedding for the day after the holiday.

"I'd rather be with friends." Prowling across the grass, Adrienne retrieved a crumpled teddy-bear birth certificate. The kids had filled them out for their stuffed animals.

"You do have plans for Thanksgiving dinner, right?" Harper asked. "We're going to eat with Peter's parents. You'd both be welcome, I'm sure."

"I'm on duty that night. But yes, we have plans." Those involved treating her nephew to supper at a favorite restaurant, after which he'd join his sitter and her family. While it was painful being away from him, someone had to deliver the babies. Also, the trade-off was that Adrienne didn't have to work Christmas Eve or Christmas night.

"If you're sure…" Harper stopped as childish voices drifted from an upstairs window.

"Don't open that!" Reggie shouted.

"I want to play with it," Mia answered stubbornly.

"No way! My dad gave me that."

*His dad.* The boy had already accepted Wade in that role.

It hurt, even though Adrienne knew that fathers were important. Reg used to cling to Mia's father, Sean. His death in an off-road vehicle accident had been hard on them all. Recently, Peter and Cole had grown close to Reggie, but they were both still busy adjusting to their new families and had limited time.

So many losses. Maybe she ought to be grateful that Wade seemed eager to step in, but she didn't trust him.

"I let *you* play with stuff my dad gives me," Mia responded. Although the little girl treasured the memory of her late father, she'd begun referring to Peter as her dad.

"Put it down!" Reggie sounded on the verge of a meltdown.

"Okay, okay."

"Overtired," Adrienne assessed. "Let's call it a day."

"Good idea." Harper waved to Peter, who'd just emerged from stowing tables and chairs in a storage room that opened directly to the yard. "Let's go scrape Mia off the carpet."

Soon they were gone. In the kitchen, Adrienne paused to center herself. The refrigerator hummed as if happy to be stuffed with leftovers. On a rack above the old stove, light gleamed off the copper pots and pans that she rarely used. But they'd been there as long as Adrienne could remember, and she treasured them.

With a jolt, the attorney's statement came back to her. Wade could lay claim to Reggie's half of this house if he chose to, and its contents, as well. Adrienne wasn't even close to paying off her medical school debts. There was no way she could buy him out.

*He hasn't asked for anything yet.* She'd have to be on her guard, though. All the more because of Wade's undeniably appealing masculinity, which had—much as she disliked admitting it—stirred a tantalizing physical awareness.

*Good job being attracted to the wrong guy, Adrienne. Again.*

After a disastrous engagement during her residency, she'd sworn off men for a while. Then, during her mother's final illness nearly four years ago, she'd moved in to this house to help Vicki and Reggie. Between her work schedule and their needs, Adrienne lacked the emotional energy to pursue a relationship. Not that she'd been tempted by anyone.

And she wasn't tempted now, not on any serious level. Especially since she had no idea what would happen when they met with the attorney tomorrow. Once Wade had a chance to reflect about this house and its obvious value, would he remain civil or would he show a different, greedy side?

She hoped he wasn't that kind of person, for her nephew's sake as well as hers. Like it or not, Reggie's father was going to loom large in his son's emotional landscape.

Rapid footsteps—Reggie rarely moved at any speed slower than high gear—prepared her for his arrival in the kitchen. Instead of his favorite stuffed animal or the tablet computer he used for educational games and homework, he carried the police station still wrapped in plastic.

"You want to build that in the family room?" she asked.

He clutched it tighter. "I'm saving it till my dad can play with me. On my birthday!"

Again, the word *dad* shook her, a reminder of what Wade's arrival meant: that nothing would ever be the same, that they'd have to work out an arrangement. As for the possibility of losing Reg entirely, Adrienne refused to dwell on that. Because she'd fight this man with everything she had, if it came to that.

"Okay." She hadn't planned any particular activities for Tuesday beyond a special early dinner. Her office hours started at 6:00 p.m. on Tuesdays, so even on Reggie's birthday, she had to drop him at the sitter's by 5:30 p.m.

Wade might not be thrilled about sandwiching his visit between Reggie's return from school and Adrienne's departure, but… What was it he'd said? *I'd prefer just the two of us.*

Despite the urge to maintain tight control, she recognized that doing so might antagonize the man. Maybe she should allow an unsupervised visit. Surely Wade could be trusted to deliver his son to Mary Beth Ellroy's house at a reasonable hour.

Reggie broke into her reflections. "What's for dinner, Aunt Addie?"

"Aren't you stuffed?" She hadn't kept track of what he'd eaten earlier, though. In his excitement, he might have left most of the food on his plate.

"I'm hungry."

Time to turn back into Mommy, Adrienne thought as she opened the refrigerator. "Lots of sandwiches and veggies, and cake and ice cream for dessert."

"Yay!" Her nephew pulled his step stool from under the sink and stood on it to retrieve his favorite plate and cup from a cabinet. Slightly chipped, they belonged to a beloved set that had been in the family for generations.

Sooner or later everything would belong to Reggie. Unable to have children of her own, Adrienne had taken for granted that he would grow up here, secure in her love and his inheritance.

A pang twisted through her. *I won't lose him. I can't.*

She ducked her head, refusing to let Reg see her distress. Tomorrow she and Reg's father were meeting with the attorney.

She just hoped Wade Hunter didn't intend to spring any unpleasant surprises.

AFTER THE AIRINESS of the Cavill house, Daryl's apartment felt cramped and dark. Wade didn't mind the worn furniture and nearly bare shelves, which he dusted before putting away the food he'd bought, yet he couldn't help contrasting the place to Adrienne's comfortable home.

When he'd imagined bringing his son to live with him, he'd had a vague idea about them settling into a buddy-type relationship, the way he and Daryl had during his teen years, after Mom had left. The reality of a six-year-old boy was another matter entirely.

"Sorry about the food situation," remarked his father. "Working two jobs, I don't have time to cook." The oil stains on Daryl's hands testified to the weekdays he put in as a mechanic at Phil's Garage, in addition to his duties as apartment manager.

"You eat mostly fast food?" That might explain his father's thick waistline and sallow complexion.

"While you fix three-course meals?"

"I try out a recipe now and then." Wade also stocked salad fixings. Still, he was hardly a model of healthy nutrition, he conceded as he arranged boxes of cereal and pasta along with canned food.

"Those for your kid?"

"I wasn't planning to…" He stopped. Bringing Reggie here struck him as a bad idea, or at least an awkward one, yet the boy *should* meet his grandfather. "Listen, his birthday's Tuesday. You interested in getting together?"

Conflicting emotions played across the deep-etched lines of Daryl's face. "That's a lot for the kid to take in, considering he's only just met his father."

"So?" Wade wasn't sure why he pressed the issue, since he didn't relish introducing his father to Adrienne at this touchy stage of their negotiations. But Reggie was part of two families. He'd been kept away from this side of his heritage too long.

"That woman drove you out of town." Daryl's lip curled.

"Vicki?" Wade said. "She's dead."

"Yeah, well, I lost my grandson and in a lot of ways my son. Now suddenly I'm supposed to turn into warm, cuddly Grandpa. I'm not sure I have it in me."

Wade couldn't argue. While he used to wish he and his father were closer, Daryl kept his emotional barriers raised. "You didn't act like it was a big deal when I left."

"I'm not saying it was a big deal." His father opened the fridge and reached for a beer. His fingers curled, and he chose an orange soda instead.

"Okay. We won't rush it with Reggie."

"How about the old man?" That was Daryl's way of referring to Grandpa Bruce. "I'm sure he'd love having a great-grandson. You never told him about the boy, did you?"

"No. You didn't, either?"

"I figured it was your call."

"He had a low enough opinion of me without adding unwed father to the list." Although Wade and his grandfather had still been on speaking terms when Wade left Safe Harbor, their relationship had always been tinged with criticism and blame.

Despite above-average grades, Wade hadn't been a good enough student to please Grandpa. The truth was, he'd been distracted by the turmoil at home. There'd been his parents' divorce, his mother's death and Daryl's moody nature. Also, some late-night calls to pick up his father when Daryl was too inebriated to get behind the wheel.

When Bruce heard about one such rescue, he'd accused his grandson of enabling Daryl's drinking. While that might have been true, a son owed his dad loyalty. Plus, by preventing Daryl from driving under the influence, Wade had kept his only remaining parent out of jail. So when Vicki's pregnancy had come to light, Wade had assumed Grandpa would see that as yet another example of his weak character.

Thinking about his grandfather reminded him of Patty's news. "How come you never mentioned that Grandpa sold Fact Hunter?"

Moving to the living room, Daryl sank onto the couch. "You guys were on the outs, so why bother?"

Wade followed him in. "Now that I'm here, he's sure to find out about my son. I should tell him before he hears it somewhere else."

"It's up to you."

"How's his health?" In his mid-seventies, Bruce Hunter suffered from a bad cough due to years of smoking.

"Good enough for him to have a girlfriend." Daryl's finger tapped the TV remote. "He brings his car into the garage, and she picked him up once."

"What's she like?"

"Female." He clicked on the TV and switched channels to watch a football game.

That ended that discussion. Wade went to fetch the laundry. The conversation had reminded him of how far he'd strayed from his family. Now that he was becoming a father in every sense of the word, it was time to mend fences.

Whether his grandfather was willing to bury the hatchet, however, remained to be seen.

# Chapter Four

From the parking lot, Fact Hunter Investigations looked much as Wade remembered it, with a few modest upgrades. In the windows of the second-floor office, almond-colored blinds had replaced his grandfather's gold curtains, while on the street-level door, the firm's name had been stenciled in a more modern font. The entrance, which led directly to a staircase, was wedged between two other establishments: the Sexy Over Sixty Gym and, where an escrow office used to be, an electronics repair shop.

He recalled that the stairs were steep, with a freight elevator available for the handicapped. However, Grandpa used to say that most clients preferred to conduct business by phone and the internet or to have a detective pay an office or home visit.

Once, the prospect of entering that building as an employee had loomed like a prison sentence. He associated P.I. agencies with retired or partially disabled officers, not young men eager for the challenges of police work. Plus, the idea of being under his grandfather's thumb would have been enough to send Wade fleeing even had he not already held the position in Pine Tree.

Now Bruce's ownership was gone, and so was the job up north. Wade had emailed his résumé to Mike Aaron last night and to his surprise had received an immediate response inviting him to drop by for an interview. "Just phone first," the new co-owner had written.

Wade's hand went to his pocket, cupping the bulge of his mobile. And missing the weight of his service weapon.

He wasn't ready to place the call. Instead, he put the car in gear and drove out of the lot, heading south toward the ocean.

Bruce Hunter's condominium complex occupied bluffs above the harbor. Emerging from his sports coupe, Wade drew in a deep breath of salt air and tilted his face to the autumn sunlight. Seagulls mewed overhead, while below the bluffs traffic hummed along a highway. Less than a quarter mile farther south, boats bobbed at anchor in neat rows extending from a curving wharf. A few sails dotted the waters of the harbor.

He'd missed living near the ocean. While Pine Tree's mountainous locale had provided a beautiful setting for hiking and exploring, this was Wade's native habitat. All the same, he was far from certain of his welcome.

Dropping in unannounced might be tempting fate or, more likely, his grandfather's temper. Wade might even catch the old man in an embarrassing position with this new girlfriend. Wouldn't that be interesting?

Someone had propped open the gate. Amused to find Grandpa Bruce occupying a complex with such lax security, Wade followed a walkway to the old man's two-story unit and pressed the bell.

No response. He tried again and still heard nothing stirring. Where would his grandfather be at 10:00 a.m. on a Monday? Wade couldn't picture Grandpa hanging around a seniors' center.

From behind a screen of bushes, the thump of rubber-soled shoes reached his ears. Bruce Hunter came into view, sweat darkening his California Angels T-shirt and athletic shorts hanging loose on the old man's bony frame. Gray hair laced with black clung to his scalp.

He slowed his pace, studying Wade coolly. "Figured you'd drop by sooner or later." His voice had a dry rasp.

"Daryl told you I was here?"

His grandfather took out his key. "Nope. This is a small town."

Wade stepped aside, disappointed at losing the element of surprise. As usual, Bruce had the upper hand.

The door opened into a living room almost military in its neatness. The brown couch and tan carpet were freshly vacuumed, while the carved wooden cabinets and chest were buffed to a sheen. They had belonged to Wade's grandmother, who'd brought them from Germany when she married.

Karlotta Hunter had been buried before he was born, so he knew little of her except that she'd met Bruce while he was stationed in her country and had died when their son was in college. The official story was that she'd awakened late at night, tripped on the staircase, fallen and hit her head. The unofficial story, from Daryl, was that due to her unhappy marriage, she'd taken to drink, which had contributed to the accident.

Alcoholism ran deep in this family. It had skipped Bruce, although he had his own compulsion: chain-smoking. Apparently he'd quit, though, since the place no longer reeked of tobacco.

Wade settled on a polite greeting. "You look well."

"I look dirty and smell worse." His grandfather started up the steps. "Help yourself to coffee. There's no beer."

At 10:00 a.m.? The old man was assuming the worst, but Wade didn't bother to correct him. "Thanks."

He took his coffee black in a souvenir mug from Catalina Island. From a day trip with the girlfriend, perhaps? Over the buffet in the dining room, Wade studied the array of framed photos, hoping for a glimpse of the new lady, but these were all familiar faces.

Grandma Karlotta had sad eyes and old-fashioned braids wrapped around her head. A young black-haired Bruce stood stiffly erect in his blue dress marine uniform. Daryl at about the same age sported a combat utility uniform, better known as camouflage. At his college graduation, Wade posed in mortarboard and gown. There was no picture of Wade's mother.

Upstairs the shower ran for about a minute, followed by a brief fit of coughing. It ended quickly and sounded less alarming than in the old days.

Bruce descended within minutes, his pants and shirt pressed, his hair slick. "Guess you've got some news for me," he said without preamble.

How much had he heard via the grapevine? "About my son?" Wade asked.

The old man's nostrils flared. "The one you abandoned."

How typical of him to state that as fact rather than a question. "No, I didn't. His mother threatened to file false abuse charges. She was…troubled." Wade saw no reason to go into detail. "I've been paying child support."

Bruce's scowl eased. "Glad to hear you aren't a deadbeat."

*And I'd have appreciated your not assuming the worst.* Wade hadn't come here to fight, however. "I figured you might like to meet your great-grandson once I get visitation squared away with his aunt."

"His aunt?" From the refrigerator, Bruce took out a glass bottle of orange juice. "You're his father. Don't be a weakling. Take your son and tell her to get lost."

Wade hung on to his temper. "I'll handle this my way."

"Suit yourself." Bruce poured juice into a glass. "Yeah, I'd like to meet the little guy, whenever this aunt snaps her fingers and gives you permission."

"I'm here to make peace, but that isn't going to happen if you keep insulting me." Wade poured the remaining half of his coffee in the sink. It was decaf anyway.

Avoiding his gaze, his grandfather peered at a framed California Angels team photo on the wall. It bore half a dozen signatures from the players. "You tossed off a few insults of your own the last time we met."

Had he? "Such as?"

"Called me a rent-a-cop, for one thing," Bruce snarled.

"Sorry about that." Wade had lashed out in the heat of the moment.

"Your apology is too late." Resentment that must have been festering all this time blazed from his grandfather's face. "I had to sell the agency I spent years building because my son's a drunk and my grandson holds me in contempt."

Behind the anger, Wade sensed the hurt. "I don't hold you in contempt. And you never told me the future of the agency was on the line."

"I shouldn't have had to."

"I'm not a mind reader," Wade said. "Now I'd like to let bygones be bygones."

"Why? Because you need a job?" Bruce fired back. "Guess you're not too proud to be a rent-a-cop now."

"Guess I'm not."

That stopped his grandfather. "You're applying there?"

"Already have," Wade said.

They faced each other across the kitchen. If he'd thought it would do any good, Wade would have repeated that he hoped they could reconcile, but he should have known better. He'd tried to smooth things over before and it hadn't worked then, either.

After their argument he'd sent his grandfather Christmas cards despite receiving none in return. Then last December his card had come back with Bruce's address crossed out and the handwritten notation "Don't know him and don't want to."

Some people liked to hold a grudge. *Don't be one of them,* Wade told himself, and took the plunge. "I was thinking that you, me and Reggie could see a baseball game sometime."

"Maybe." If Bruce longed to meet the boy—which he probably did—he disguised it well. "Do me a favor, will you?"

"What's that?"

"Since you wouldn't stoop to work at the agency when I owned it, don't insult me by doing it now just because you got fired."

"Laid off," Wade corrected.

"Whatever, as you young people like to say."

"I'll take it under consideration." If he stayed here any longer, Wade might lose his temper the way he had during their last meeting. "See you around, Grandpa. Thanks for the coffee."

"See you." Bruce walked him to the front. From the corner of his eye, Wade saw his grandfather watching as he rounded the side of the building.

At Fact Hunter Investigations, Wade reflected, he had an excellent shot at a suitable position that would allow him to stay near Reggie. Despite the old man's request, it seemed unlikely that passing it up would do any good. More likely, his grandpa would see compliance as a weakness.

You couldn't please him, so why try? On his cell phone, Wade pressed Mike Aaron's number.

SEATED IN THE attorney's waiting room, Adrienne glanced irritably at her watch. Wade was ten minutes late, and she had to be home in an hour to meet Reggie's school bus.

Doubts and speculation were driving her crazy. In her medical practice, she was accustomed to dealing with uncertainty. Patient outcomes couldn't always be predicted, and in surgery she had to change tactics instantly if complications developed.

Yet she'd lain awake last night, struggling with the unknowns about Reggie's father. Would he break his son's heart by playing the doting daddy until he got bored? Or would he demand full custody, ignoring Reggie's attachment to Adrienne? In either case, what about Reggie's rights to the house and its contents?

The man was no knuckle-dragging Neanderthal, Adrienne conceded. But she'd grown up with a bipolar father whose mood swings had kept the household teetering on the brink between his warm, expansive side and his abrupt withdrawals. Her sister had been equally unpredictable. There was no telling how many sides Wade Hunter had or which would emerge today.

Then she saw him through the blinds, cutting across the parking lot. He was carrying… Were those flowers?

She barely had time to rise and smooth her powder-blue dress before he blew into the room on a crisp breeze. Wearing a dark suit, with a trace of early gray at the temples, he had a distinguished air offset by the apologetic gleam in his eyes.

He regarded her appreciatively. "I like your hair down. That's a good color on you, too."

Adrienne rarely wore dresses and usually put her hair in a twist or ponytail. Nervous about this meeting, she'd taken extra care today. "Thanks. Listen…"

"I didn't mean to be late." Wade held out a decorative pot containing a yellow miniature rose. With shiny green leaves and copious buds, it would fit perfectly into her front bed. "Just landed a job, and on my way from the interview, I passed a flower shop. It occurred to me that a peace offering might be appropriate."

"I love miniature roses. Thank you." A peace offering—

better than hostility, in Adrienne's opinion. Then the rest of his statement registered. "You're going to work at the police department?"

"Private agency. Fact Hunter."

"Congratulations." Clearly, Wade didn't plan to leave town soon. That might be good…or not. It meant less of a likelihood that her little boy would be carted away to some distant place, yet having his father living nearby was far from ideal.

The inner door opened. Geoff Humphreys emerged, greeting Adrienne before turning to the new arrival. "Mr. Hunter? Pleased to meet you in person."

"Me, too."

After shaking hands, they went into the comfortably appointed office. "Did I hear you say you found a job at Fact Hunter?" the attorney asked.

"Founded by my grandfather, although if there's an opposite to nepotism, that's what I have." In an upholstered chair, Wade sat straight with legs slightly apart, as if accustomed to a heavy equipment belt. Adrienne had seen Patty sit the same way.

"Mike Aaron owns it now, doesn't he?" Geoff didn't explain how he knew that.

Wade tilted his head in acknowledgment. "That's right."

"Mike's wife is a colleague of mine," Adrienne put in. "Dr. Paige Brennan."

Wade blinked. "A cop and a doctor? That's an unusual combination."

"It's not uncommon around here. Patty's married to an embryologist, Alec Denny, although he's a Ph.D., not an M.D." In case that sounded snobbish, she added, "As Alec keeps reminding everyone."

"What about this brother of Mike Aaron's?" Wade said. "Ever meet him? I like to know who I'm working for."

"Lock's a good guy," Adrienne told him. "He married

a surgical nurse, Erica. They have a little boy—almost a year old."

"Does this town put something in the water?" he asked. "Seems like everybody's getting married and having kids."

"We're a friendly bunch." Despite her attempt at a light tone, Adrienne felt an all-too-familiar tensing in the gut at the reminder that she would never be so lucky. She was grateful when Geoff cleared his throat, drawing their attention to the topic at hand.

"While I realize you're just getting acquainted, we should discuss a parenting plan," he said. "That describes how parents will handle a variety of practical matters in their child's life. It prevents misunderstandings and minimizes conflict."

"We could all use more of that," Wade muttered as Geoff handed out printed sheets. "Minimizing conflict, I mean."

Adrienne scanned the list. Although she appreciated order, she found it daunting. It called for plans regarding visitation, both regular and for vacations and holidays, instructions as to dietary requirements and internet use, details of how to handle contact with extended family members and parents' dating partners, and numerous other issues. "Is this really necessary?"

"It will be eventually," Geoff said. "We don't have to carve anything in stone right now."

"This visitation business," Wade put in. "I don't know my work schedule yet."

"I can imagine your hours might be somewhat irregular," the lawyer noted. "Perhaps you'd be willing to stipulate that you accept Dr. Cavill's current babysitting arrangements."

Adrienne could see Wade's muscles tightening. "Is that a problem for you?" she asked him.

"I haven't met the babysitter yet."

How dare he question her choices? Adrienne gripped

the pot in her lap. Peace offering or not, she was tempted to chuck it at Wade's head.

Yet as Geoff had warned earlier, antagonizing the man was likely to backfire. She'd done research on the internet, hoping to find that Vicki's will and Adrienne's longtime care of Reggie put her in the driver's seat. To her dismay, the articles she'd read had confirmed that Wade's rights took precedence over hers.

She'd been shocked to discover that in California and many other states, even rapists could sue for child custody and/or visitation. Considering that Wade was the injured party here due to Vicki's threats toward him, what chance was there that a court would side with Adrienne?

That didn't mean she was giving up on maintaining primary custody. But she'd have to win over Wade with diplomacy, not temper tantrums.

"You should consider living arrangements," Geoff persisted. "What about overnight visitation, for instance?"

"I'm sleeping on my father's couch, so I can hardly take Reggie home with me." Wade shook his head. "I'm not ready to work out a parenting plan. It sounds like a good idea for later, though."

"I don't mind if we play this by ear for a while." In time, Adrienne thought, Wade might accept that staying with her was in his son's best interest.

"To a certain extent, that may be necessary," the lawyer said. "However—"

"What about this business of supervised visits?" Wade pressed. "I don't see why I can't spend time alone with my son."

The attorney frowned. "You *are* a stranger to him."

Wade leaned forward, storm clouds gathering in his expression. This could blow up in her face, Adrienne realized. Besides, she'd already considered the matter, so why quarrel about it?

She raised her hand in a stop gesture. "It's fine with me if Wade wants to have private time with Reggie tomorrow evening. My office hours start at six, and he's looking forward to assembling that toy police station with his dad."

As she spoke, Wade nodded. It felt almost as if they were on the same side.

"Toy police station? Did I miss something?" Geoff asked.

She explained about Wade stopping by the birthday party. "They aren't strangers anymore. I'm comfortable with an unsupervised visit. I'm sure my nephew will be fine."

Wade's pleased expression lasted only seconds before he broached another subject. "That sounds good, but won't you be at the hospital all night? Does that mean I should sleep over?"

Adrienne hadn't thought of that possibility and didn't care for it. "His regular sitter, Mary Beth Ellroy, and her family are planning a celebration for Reggie—cake and a few small presents. If you could drop him off at her house around eight, that would be great. That'll give you a chance to meet them, too."

Relief spread across his face. "That's reasonable."

"Good." Adrienne indicated Geoff's paper. "This is an excellent starting point for discussion as we get situated."

"Very well." The lawyer tapped his finger on the desk blotter. "I should caution Mr. Hunter that at first, children's schedules may feel unduly restrictive. My wife and I have two youngsters, and between their activities and her job as a teacher, it feels like we're conducting army maneuvers on a daily basis."

"I grew up in a chaotic home," Wade said. "With more order and stability, I'd have been a better student. My grandfather, by contrast, would have had me doing push-ups at five-thirty every morning and saluting when he walked by. There has to be a happy medium."

Adrienne agreed. Was it possible she and this man could work together long-term to co-parent Reggie? She didn't relish the idea of sharing control, but it might be her only option. And perhaps not as bad as she'd feared.

"Let's meet with Geoff again in a couple weeks," she suggested. "By then we'll have a better handle on things."

The men concurred. As she rose to leave, Adrienne checked her watch. "It's almost time to meet Reggie's school bus." Impulsively, she added, "Wade, would you like to come?"

His frown lines vanished. "Very much. I start work on Wednesday, so I won't have many free afternoons."

Maybe she was certifiable, Adrienne mused as she left. Still, he'd brought her the potted rose, and she might as well meet him halfway.

They drove off in their separate cars. During the short trip, Adrienne's brain buzzed with considerations, including the likelihood that once he began receiving paychecks, Wade would rent a place and expect overnight visits. Well, they'd take that step when they came to it.

*As long as he leaves Reggie with me.* If not… She didn't dare finish that sentence.

In front of her house, she found his sporty black coupe parked at the curb. He was leaning against it, more than sexy enough to match the car's image.

*Don't you dare think like that.*

"I know of a few upcoming vacancies that might interest you, if you're looking for a rental," she told him as they stood on the walkway together.

"You double as a real estate agent?" Wade joked.

"I suppose I'm compulsive about putting people's lives in order," Adrienne admitted. "Plus, you'll want a safe place for Reggie where he'd be comfortable. For overnights."

"That's thoughtful of you."

"Practical, really." Down the block, Adrienne saw a couple mothers waiting at the corner bus stop. Since she'd rather speak without an audience, she remained in place. "My friends Stacy and Cole opened escrow on a house, and they'll be vacating their apartment in a month. Then Harper and Peter are getting married at Thanksgiving, and she's leaving her rental house."

He ran a hand over his short thick hair. "I'd love to get off Dad's couch, but I'm watching my wallet."

"You don't have to pay for Reggie's upkeep," she blurted.

His eyes narrowed. "I'm his father. Of course I'll help support him."

"Sorry." Adrienne hadn't meant to step into a minefield. "I was just…"

"Trying to let me off the hook?" Wade asked.

"If that's what you want." *Please say yes.*

"It isn't."

"Understood." Maybe Geoff had been right. This discussion might have been easier with an objective third party. On the other hand, the attorney had put Wade's back up, too.

The rumble of the bus approaching on the cross street short-circuited further discussion. They went to join the small group of parents waiting for their kids.

THE IDEA THAT he might stop paying his son's support had made Wade bristle. Walking beside Adrienne toward the corner, however, he conceded that she was trying to be generous. Just because his grandfather always expected the worst of him didn't mean she did.

He could see now that being a father required a lot of planning. In Pine Tree he'd had a one-bedroom unit, but that might feel crowded if Reggie slept over. Also, Wade's usual mode of decorating, or rather not decorating, wasn't exactly kid oriented.

He wished he had a house like Adrienne's, with its well-stocked kitchen, cozy furnishings and vegetable garden. While Wade didn't plan for his relationship with Reggie to turn into a competition, neither did he care to make a poor showing.

What did other single fathers do? Did they buy toy chests and bunk beds and all that stuff? When he rented a place, maybe Adrienne could advise him on how to set it up. That is, if she remained as cooperative as she'd been today.

While she obviously wasn't thrilled about having Wade around, she appeared to understand that the law favored his claim. And for his part, it didn't take a lot of parenting experience to see that yanking a little boy out of his home and away from the woman who anchored his world would be an act of selfishness, not love. Like it or not, they were stuck with each other, for now.

Ahead, the yellow bus halted, lights blinking, and a stop arm extending from the left side. The door wheezed open. Two girls got off, followed by a boy of about ten. Then a familiar head of blond hair appeared.

When Reggie saw Wade, surprise flashed across his face, then a smile. "Dad?"

"Hey, kid. Thought I'd drop by."

"Yeah!" Reg jumped down and trotted over, backpack bouncing. His heart expanding, Wade bent to share a hug.

The three of them strolled to the house, Reggie in the middle holding both their hands. "I'm only staying for a few minutes today," Wade said. Adrienne hadn't invited him to dinner, and there was no reason she should. "I'll be back tomorrow for your birthday, and we can build that police set."

Reggie slanted a disappointed glance up at him. "You aren't staying?"

Since it would be unfair to lay the blame on Adrienne,

Wade replied, "I have a lot to do. I'm starting a new job Wednesday. I need to buy a couple suits and, uh, figure out where to live." *Eventually.*

They reached the front walk. "You can stay with us," Reggie offered. "We have plenty of room."

Adrienne gave a start. "Honey, we can't just invite someone to move in."

"Why not?" the little boy demanded. "You told me I own half the house. And I want my dad to live here."

# Chapter Five

A sharp refusal sprang to Adrienne's lips. This stranger, this interloper, this dangerously attractive man, move into her house?

But although she was accustomed to taking charge at the hospital and with her nephew, so much hung in the balance. Wade could side with his son, casting her as the enemy. Even if not, she risked offending him unnecessarily.

Over Reggie's head, their eyes met. Did he read her panic? Embarrassed, Adrienne searched for diplomatic words. "It's not that simple."

"Your aunt isn't running a motel," Wade told Reggie. "I can't just dump my stuff at her place and interrupt her routine. Besides, we all have to get used to me being your dad. Let's take this slow, okay?"

*That was decent of him.* When they reached the front porch, Adrienne fished the keys from her purse, grateful for the excuse to avert her face. If Wade saw her expression, he might notice how relieved she felt. And the last thing she wanted was pity.

"Peter's going to live with Mia and her mommy," Reggie protested. "He's not even her real dad."

"He and Mia's mother are getting married," Wade reminded him. "That's a special relationship."

Storm clouds gathered in the little boy's eyes. "What if I don't get to see you?"

The topic had shifted, thank goodness. "You'll be spending plenty of time with your dad," Adrienne said.

"Tomorrow night, for instance," Wade put in.

Reggie stood with feet planted apart. "If you lived here, you won't disappear."

Her nephew's anxiety was well-grounded, Adrienne conceded sadly. Not only had he lived all these years without a father, but Reggie had also lost his mother and grandmother, as well as Mia's father. In his small world, loved ones did indeed disappear, never to return.

"I *do* live here now," Wade countered. "In Safe Harbor. I've been hired at a detective agency, which means I'm staying. I'm your father, and you can count on me being around from now on."

Adrienne found that prospect worrisome. Still, things could have gone worse had Wade tried to move into the house.

Well, they had a routine to stick to. After opening the door, she said, "Let's have a look at your homework, Reg."

"I don't want to do homework!" Seeing her frown, the little boy amended that to, "I'll do it later."

"After dinner Peter promised to shoot hoops with you and Mia while Harper and I shop for wedding stuff, remember?" Adrienne said. "Let's get it out of the way."

Reggie grabbed his father's hand as they went into the front hall. "Dad, will you help?"

"Sure, if… What kind of homework is it?" Wade asked.

"The first-grade kind," Adrienne teased.

Wade gazed fondly at his son's eager face. "I can add one plus one. Let's get started."

Reggie reached into his backpack. He stopped, his hand in midair. "Oops."

"You left it at school?" Adrienne would have to check the teacher's website.

"No. I forgot." Reggie wrinkled his nose. "I don't have any homework today."

How typical of her nephew to stand his ground, ready to fight to the bitter end about something that didn't exist. "Lucky for you," she said. "You can play. Something educational."

"That gives me an idea. Hang on." Slipping free, Wade strode down the steps and went to his car. Reggie took off in pursuit.

Adrienne nearly ran after him until she saw him stop on the sidewalk. They weren't driving away, for heaven's sake.

From the trunk, Wade lifted a guitar case. "Do you know what this is?" His voice carried across the lawn.

The boy studied it warily. "It's a machine gun."

"What?"

As the man swung toward Adrienne in confusion, she started to laugh. "Too many gangster shows on TV," she said as they neared her.

"Aha." Wade regarded his son in amusement. "Reg, it's a guitar."

"Like in a rock band?"

"Yes, except rock bands use electric guitars. This one is acoustic. It has a softer sound."

In the den Reggie perched on the sofa beside his father. Despite the difference in hair color—Wade's was medium brown, Reggie's blond—the rounded shapes of their heads showed a strong resemblance.

The little boy watched in fascination as Wade took out a small electronic device and began tightening the strings. "What's that?"

"It's a tuner," he explained as he worked. "Centuries ago somebody decided it's easier to sing and play music with other people if we all use the same notes. Like, not too high and not too low." His voice rose to a squeak on *high* and dropped to bass on *low*.

Reggie giggled.

"We use letters from A to G to identify the notes," Wade said. "Each string is assigned a particular note, but they get loose on their pegs, so they have to be tuned."

"How can you tell which is which?" Reggie asked.

"On a guitar the lowest string is usually tuned to an E. The others are A, D, G, B and then E again, an octave higher. That's… Well, let's keep this simple. One more thing—when I strum more than one string at a time, that's called a chord."

"Can't I just play it?" the little boy asked.

"Anything worth doing is worth doing well," Wade replied, bending over his instrument. "Just as you learn arithmetic and reading and geography, musicians learn about notes and chords."

He was a natural teacher, Adrienne reflected. And patient, at least under these relaxed circumstances. Was it possible things could continue this smoothly? *Stay alert just in case.*

Tuneful strumming broke into her thoughts. Adrienne recognized the opening notes of "Teddy Bears' Picnic."

"If you go into the woods today…" Wade's mellow tenor captured the spirit of the song. Reggie joined in enthusiastically, and after a moment, Adrienne couldn't resist singing, too.

When the song ended, Reggie said, "I'll be right back!" Out he raced, feet thumping on the stairs.

"What's he up to?" Wade asked.

"I'm sure we'll find out in a few milliseconds." From her chair Adrienne leaned toward him, drawn by Wade's openness. "How did you learn that song?"

"After I heard it at your house, I found it on the internet."

He'd done research and put forth the effort to learn it, she reflected. "You play well. Did you take classes?"

"I'm self-taught." He smoothed the satiny finish of the guitar. "Thank goodness for online tutorials."

More pounding feet, and Reggie rounded the corner with his favorite teddy bear. "Zoomer wants to sing, too."

"Is this an encore request?" Wade asked. "That means a repeat."

"Yes!"

They ran through the song again, followed by several other old favorites. At five o'clock Adrienne reluctantly ended the session. "It's time to fix dinner. Reggie, you need to set the table."

"You do it," the little boy grumbled.

"That's no way to talk to your aunt." Wade replaced the guitar in its case. "I'll teach you a few chords tomorrow if you like, but you have to obey your aunt."

He was standing up for her. Adrienne hadn't expected that.

"Okay." Reggie's face scrunched, a sign that his brain was working hard. Adrienne tensed. His schemes could be unpredictable, like inviting Wade to live here. "Dad?"

"What, little guy?" Wade rumpled his son's hair.

"Will you sleep over Friday night?" Reggie asked. "My sitter's having out-of-town guests."

"You're staying with Aunt Stacy and Uncle Cole on Friday," Adrienne reminded him.

"Aunt Stacy gets tired. You said so yourself," Reggie argued.

"Tell you what," Wade replied. "You take Zoomer up to your room and wash your hands for dinner. Your aunt and I will discuss this."

Deep breath, a wiggle on the sofa and Reggie yielded. "Okay. But say yes, Aunt Addie."

Adrienne felt torn. While yielding might encourage Reggie's demands for his father to move in, she disliked repeatedly saying no. "Once he gets an idea in his head, it sticks like glue," she observed after the boy left.

"So I'm learning." The dimming light through the bay window cast Wade in partial shadow, silhouetting the breadth of his shoulders and bringing out the strong lines of his face. "Look, I understand that I'm the shiny new toy in his life, but you're the one he depends on."

"Seriously?" Adrienne asked.

Wade's eyebrows drew together. "You think I'm just saying that? Like I have some ulterior motive?"

"I didn't mean it that way."

"Let's be clear. I'm not abdicating my authority over my son," he said. "The law's on my side, according to my research, but at this age a boy needs a mother, too, and you're doing a great job of standing in for his. Probably better than she did. For his sake, I'm willing to work together."

"So am I, but…" Usually, Adrienne guarded her emotions carefully, but this man's openness deserved candor on her part, too. "Nothing personal. I'm just not sure how far I trust anyone, emotionally."

"Even your friends?"

*Good question.* "Stacy and Harper were Vicki's friends first. They kept her afloat as best they could, and now they're helping Reg and me. I don't know what I'd do without them. All the same…" Deeply thankful for their support, she'd never stopped to question how far she could rely on them.

"But you don't feel completely safe with anyone." Wade rested an elbow on the upright guitar case.

"Yes." She'd held that truth inside, unwilling to admit it to those close to her. "How can you understand that?"

"As I mentioned, I grew up in a chaotic home," he said. "My father's an alcoholic. It's like what people say about the weather. If you don't like your parent's mood, just wait a few minutes."

Her father and sister had been mercurial, too. "That applies equally to my upbringing. I learned not to trust promises."

"For the record, I don't entirely trust you, either." When he smiled, the fading light glinted off his white teeth.

"You think I'll turn on you?"

"If I do or say the wrong thing, possibly."

This was the bluntest discussion Adrienne ever recalled having—certainly with a man. "Where does that leave us?"

Overhead, the water stopped running. Reggie had finished washing his hands.

"Let's make this a win-win situation," Wade proposed. "I'll pitch in Friday night. With my new job, I can't promise to be a regular weekend sitter, but you deserve a break, and so does your pregnant friend."

"Is this a foot in the door?" she asked.

Wade shook his head. "No, it's a bedroll in the den. And if there are any dripping faucets that need fixing, stuff like that, let me know so I can pick up supplies."

"I'm fairly competent with a wrench. But that's kind of you." Adrienne felt obligated to add, "You're turning out to be a better father than I expected."

"Really? Mostly I'm going by instinct." He ran his hand over the gentle curve of the guitar case. "In view of my family experiences, it's good to hear that I'm not screwing this up."

"You aren't," she confirmed.

His eyes met hers with a tingle of electricity. "That was hard for you to say, wasn't it?"

"Horribly." He was very perceptive—scarily so. "Reggie means everything to me."

"That makes two of us." Wade arose as his son pelted in.

"Well?" Reg demanded, wiping his damp hands on his jeans. "You can stay here on Friday, right?"

"Hey, sport, here's the deal." Wade fixed him with a

stare. "Tomorrow night for your birthday I'll take you and your aunt out for an early dinner and play with you till around eight. Then we'll go to your sitter's. On Friday I can stay over."

"Yay!" The little boy jumped in the air.

It hurt to see him so eager to be with his father, and Adrienne had to fight the impulse to reassert control. Still, she recognized the inevitability of sharing power with Wade, like it or not. Besides, after their conversation, she didn't *dislike* it as much as she had before.

"There are conditions," Wade went on.

Reggie stopped jumping.

"You have to help your aunt around the house and treat her with respect. Just because I'm here doesn't mean she's been demoted, okay?"

"Okay," Reggie agreed, although Adrienne doubted he knew what *demoted* meant.

"I refuse to provide an excuse for misbehavior," Wade concluded. "So do me proud. Show your aunt what a great kid you are, and you'll be showing me, too."

"Yes, Dad." Reggie laced his hands in front of him.

Having a veritable stranger defend her rights as a parent felt strange. *I don't need anyone's help,* was Adrienne's first reaction. Yet kids naturally tested limits, and it helped when both parents backed each other up.

"Now, I have to leave," Wade told his son. "Didn't I hear someone mention setting the table?"

"I will!" Reggie scampered toward the kitchen. That was impressive cooperation, Adrienne mused.

Wade tilted his head. "Not even a hug for poor old Dad."

"One-track mind." And a reminder that Wade wouldn't always be—what had he called himself?—the shiny new toy.

After arranging to pick her and Reggie up the next day

at four-thirty, he went into the kitchen and said goodbye to his son. Then he was gone.

As she punched in Stacy's number to cancel Friday's plans, Adrienne sensed that matters were slipping from her hands. But only a little. And that didn't scare her nearly as much as she would have expected.

ON TUESDAY WADE bought new clothes in preparation for his job. Aside from a sports coat and dress pants to wear to interviews, he'd neglected his wardrobe, if you could apply that term to a well-worn assortment of jeans, chinos, T-shirts and polos.

At lunch he arranged to meet a trio of high school friends. After they reminisced about sports and teachers, the conversation shifted to their families. One fellow was divorced with a little girl, another happily married without kids and the third living with a woman with whom he had two children.

They offered advice that ranged from the insightful—don't rush closeness, children need a chance to bond—to the cynical—watch out for the woman, she'll try to get her hands on your money. As if he had any. Wade departed little wiser than when he'd arrived. Still, he was glad to be back in town. Despite not keeping in touch with his friends since he'd left Safe Harbor, all those years of growing up together had forged a bond that would always be there.

The discovery that he'd missed Safe Harbor forced him to reflect on how hard it would be on Reggie to leave. Still, the boy was only six. If necessary, they'd go…but Wade would prefer if this job worked out.

And he couldn't deny Adrienne's role as a mother figure for Reggie. She bore little resemblance to her sister. More like Wade, she'd evidently been the responsible kid in a dysfunctional family.

Their ties to Reggie might keep him and Adrienne in

close contact for years. That prospect pleased him, despite the potential for conflict. She was, in her way, a kindred spirit. In her less prickly moods, he liked her. Perhaps even *during* her prickly moods.

At his father's apartment Wade was preparing to go out for his son's birthday dinner when Daryl stomped in, smelling of motor oil even though he appeared to have washed. This morning when Wade had told him about taking the job at Fact Hunter, he'd merely nodded. Now, indicating a garment bag bearing the name of a men's store, he said, "So what does the well-dressed detective wear these days?"

"Something dignified and low-key." Wade hadn't meant to leave his purchases draped over the couch. "I'll put that away."

"Whatever you bought, I'm sure it beats a blue jumpsuit." Daryl must have left that at the garage, though, since he was wearing jeans and a loose shirt.

"Protects your clothes."

"Yeah, that's true." While his father went into the kitchen, Wade hung his purchases in the front closet. Daryl returned carrying a beer. "Told the old man about your new position yet?"

"I'll let him find out via the grapevine." Wade suspected the agency's receptionist kept in touch with her longtime boss. "I'd rather avoid him till he's had a chance to get used to the idea."

"Think you'll live that long?" His father downed a swallow from the can before adding, "He should be glad you're working in your field."

"More or less."

Daryl scowled at an oil stain on the back of his hand. "Look at me. A mechanic and a handyman."

"Honorable professions," Wade said quietly. "And useful."

His father sank onto the couch. "Another year nearly

gone. Glad my son's back, but other than that..." The sentence trailed off.

Wade decided against mentioning his grandson. It was too volatile a subject when his dad was in a mood like this. Instead, being familiar with his father's emotional patterns, he searched for a way to cut short what might become a spiral into depression—and heavier drinking. "What do you and Grandpa usually do for Thanksgiving? Maybe we can plan something."

"Fight," Daryl responded succinctly.

Wade hoped that was an exaggeration. "Every year?"

"We used to. Nowadays we just give it a miss."

Too bad they'd quit trying. "Where do you eat, then?"

"They make pretty good frozen turkey dinners these days."

"You're not eating a frozen dinner on Thanksgiving this year." Too late, Wade reflected how lonely it was, dining in a restaurant on holidays, which was why he usually volunteered at a charity kitchen. "Tell you what—I'll cook. We can watch football and stuff ourselves." He'd volunteer another day.

"I'd like that." Daryl brightened. "And that means leftovers. They're the best part. Well, almost."

"What's better than leftovers?"

"Pie," his father said. "You hadn't forgotten that, right?"

"If you don't mind store-bought."

"Fine with me."

"It's a deal," Wade said. "Got a dinner date with my boy. I'll see you later."

"Later." Daryl clicked on the TV.

Wade was glad he'd raised his father's spirits. While he wasn't sure how one baked a turkey, he'd figure it out.

Maybe he'd ask Adrienne. She ought to know.

## Chapter Six

Although he'd once sworn never to work at Fact Hunter Investigations, Wade had a sense of homecoming as he climbed the steps shortly before 9:00 a.m. on Wednesday. He knew this office well from his visits over the years with Grandpa Bruce. It felt like familiar territory.

Not that he hadn't enjoyed last night's dinner with Adrienne and little Reggie, as well as the one-on-one toy-building session that had followed. Still, he'd been dogged by a recurring sense of being out of his depth.

Busted back to a rookie. Man, he hated that feeling. But new daddies had to learn the ropes, including—when he dropped Reggie off at eight—making nice with the baby-sitter and her family, who knew his son better than he did.

At the top of the stairs, a windowed door bearing the firm's name opened into the outer office. The new owners had repainted and recarpeted, touches that were long overdue even if clients rarely visited.

One wall sported framed certificates, awards and commendations. Some had been earned by Mike Aaron during his stint as a Safe Harbor police detective and others by co-owner Lock Vaughn, whom Mike had referred to as his foster brother.

Ahead, behind the front counter, the middle-aged receptionist jumped up to greet him. "Wade! This is like old home week!" A graying divorcée who'd worked for

Grandpa practically forever, Sue Carrera had tactfully kept a low profile a few days ago when Wade had had his interview.

"For me, too." He gave her a hug. "I'm glad you're still holding down the fort."

"They'd be lost without me," Sue told him, with good reason. She'd always had an encyclopedic knowledge of the clients, handled bookkeeping as well as secretarial duties and spoke Spanish fluently, an asset in Southern California. "So not married yet?"

She also took a keen interest in other people's love lives, Wade recalled. During his younger years he'd learned never to mention a romantic entanglement in Sue's presence. "Nope."

"I've married off both the owners." She sounded as if she were personally responsible. "It's your turn next."

From the hallway, Patty Hartman—married name Patty Denny, Wade corrected mentally—swung into view. She wore a navy pantsuit that, except for the pink blouse peeping through the jacket, reminded him of a police uniform. That was clearly her comfort zone.

"Give the guy a couple weeks in town before he ties the knot, will ya?" she fired cheerfully at Sue. "Welcome on board, Wade."

They shook hands. "Thanks for the tip about the job," Wade said.

"Glad to have you. Not sure you need a tour, but here goes." Patty gestured down the hall. "Mike and Lock have private offices, while I use the report-writing room. I guess you'll be joining me."

"That's what Mike said. He also mentioned I could do some work from home, which will be convenient when I have one."

As soon as he paused, Sue spoke again. "How's your little boy? You should bring him for a visit."

"Good idea." Wade planned to leave that for later, though. "I'm still figuring out how to be a dad. There are websites for stepfathers and parents of infants, but I haven't found anything that covers my situation."

"Afraid I can't help there." Sue had never had kids.

"It's no big deal," Patty volunteered. "From my vast experience with Fiona, all it takes is being patient, fitting into their life, realizing you don't always have to be right and, let's see, don't let them pit you against the other parent."

That was reassuring since Wade had made those same observations. "I appreciate the info."

They all turned as the outer door opened to admit a powerfully built man about Wade's height with thick hair in mixed shades from blond to dark brown. Squeezing through with his laptop case and a large pink-striped bag, he cast a startled gaze at the three observers. "I'm late, huh? Jordan had a little diaper accident. You must be the new guy. Wade, right? Lock Vaughn."

Wade shook the hand that stretched out from amidst the various straps. He hoped the co-owner had washed it recently. "Glad to meet you."

"I thought Erica took your kid to the hospital day-care center," Patty said.

"Surgical nurses start duty at seven. Jordan wasn't ready." Frowning, Lock glanced down. "Oh, hell. I forgot to leave the diaper bag."

This was a father after Wade's heart. "I'm glad I'm not the only dad who feels overwhelmed."

Lock seemed to be cogitating hard about this dilemma. "They'll have to improvise till I can swing by at lunch. Erica'll kill me. Maybe not. She puts up with a lot."

The phone rang, summoning Sue to her desk. Unsure of his next step, Wade strolled behind Lock to the co-owner's office. Where Mike's had the tailored style of an executive domain, this room contained a plain desk, a filing cabinet and a couple chairs. Plus, on the walls, three paintings of the Grand Canyon at different times of day. "Cool art."

"I shipped these from Flagstaff for the waiting room," Lock said, setting the laptop on the desk. "Mike hung them just long enough to pacify my ego and then moved them in here."

"Mike has a thing about being in charge," noted Patty, who'd accompanied them. "You gotta hand it to him, though. He brings in the business and schmoozes nice with the corporate types."

That fit Wade's impression of his new boss—co-boss, really, although he was gathering that Lock didn't throw his weight around. Back in Wade's years with the local P.D., Mike had been a patrolman intent on moving up to detective. And so he had. Later, when he learned this agency was for sale, he'd seen it as a rare opportunity to have a bigger impact on the community, he'd mentioned at the interview. Wade wouldn't be surprised if the guy had long-term political ambitions.

"If you don't mind my asking, what's this about you and Mike being foster brothers?" Wade hoped it wasn't a sore subject.

Lock stuffed the diaper bag out of sight and input something to his phone—no doubt a reminder to drop it off. "I had a rough start. My birth mom turned me over to an adoptive couple who got hooked on drugs. I floated around foster care for a while till Mike's family took pity on my obnoxious self. I proceeded to make their lives miserable during my adolescence, but they loved me anyway."

"Mike was in foster care, too?"

"Him?" Patty said. "Not likely."

"He had the good judgment to be born into a caring family who took in odd lots like me." After a beat, Lock added, "Interestingly, once I moved back to Safe Harbor, I met my birth mom. She's a volunteer at the hospital and friends with Erica, which meant I had the satisfaction of receiving an apology."

"More than that. You guys are close," Patty put in.

"Yeah, it worked out." The tinge of irony was gone. "Renée—that's my birth mom, Renée Green—never had any other kids. She's a doting grandma."

The air pressure in the room shifted. Wade wasn't sure if it was the arrival of another burly man or simply the impact of Mike's presence, but he knew instantly that the real boss had stepped in.

He pivoted to greet Mike Aaron. Despite his impressive height, the guy had a low-key appearance with his tailored gray suit, sandy hair and steely eyes softened by reading glasses. All the same, his cool gaze sent an unmistakable message: *alpha male on deck.*

"Welcome aboard," Mike told Wade.

That required another declaration that he was glad to be there and another handshake. This one was so firm it almost hurt.

Patty slipped out of view. Lock sat down at his laptop.

Mike led the way to his office, where he handed Wade a printed document in a stiff cover. "Our policies and procedures." With a trace of a smile, he added, "There'll be a pop quiz later."

"No problem."

Policies and procedures, huh? While the guy was more up-to-date than Grandpa, Wade had the same uncomfortable impression of being put in his place. *Well, get over it.* Mike had a right to establish the chain of command.

A second folder followed. "Your first case. Suspected cheating wife to surveil."

"I'll get right on it." Wade started out.

"Read the rules first."

This guy was definitely cut from the same cloth as Grandpa. "I'll get right on it after I read the rules."

Mike chuckled. "Bruce trained you well."

Wade suppressed the temptation to salute. "He did his best."

In the report-writing room, Wade sat at one of three stations, each equipped with a computer. Filing cabinets and shelves neatly stacked with office supplies lined two walls, while a small window overlooked a nearby residential neighborhood.

Three stations. Mike was looking ahead.

From downstairs, rhythmic creaking noises caught his attention. Those must be the seniors at the Sexy Over Sixty Gym, or rather their equipment. Well, Wade could concentrate amid almost any sort of noise.

He opened the manual. Topics included guarding client confidentiality, obeying the law at all times, being completely honest with a client about what services they could and couldn't provide and preserving evidence in case it was needed in court.

Although none of this was new to Wade, it brought home that his focus was on the client. That included not only individuals and companies, but also lawyers who might be defending criminal cases.

Mike was right to emphasize studying the rules. At work, no matter how prepared he felt, Wade had to guard against rookie mistakes.

By comparison, spending an overnight with his son didn't pose such a challenge after all.

From 6:00 to 8:00 p.m. on Fridays, Adrienne saw private patients at her office before her overnight shift in Labor and Delivery at the hospital next door. The evening hours accommodated working women, and the income helped pay off her medical school loans faster.

Tonight her last patient was Stacy. At six months of gestation, the triplets were growing well, with no signs of distress. However, in Adrienne's opinion, their mom ought to quit trying to be superwoman and take leave from her job as Cole's surgical nurse.

"I can't imagine you enjoy standing on your feet at this stage," Adrienne observed as she helped Stacy sit up on the examining table. "Cole should insist you get more rest."

"He's learned not to boss me around outside the O.R.," her friend responded. With her mischievous smile and curly brown hair, she could have passed for a teenager. "You're right. I should put in for leave, but I'll miss this place. I like being in the middle of everything."

"Harper and I will keep you in the loop," Adrienne promised.

"Hearing about stuff isn't the same as being here," Stacy said. "Like at lunch today Zora threw a divorce party in the cafeteria. Maybe this is petty of me, but I found it highly satisfying."

Ultrasound technician Zora Raditch had stolen Stacy's first husband, Andrew. Two years later Zora had caught him cheating with someone else. In view of his untrustworthy character, that might have seemed predictable to anyone else, but she'd been devastated. Later she'd rallied, and she appeared to be taking the divorce in stride.

"You're remarkably tolerant of her." Adrienne opened the door for her friend.

"Oh, I hated her guts for a while. Then I realized she did me a favor." Stacy chuckled. "Andrew doesn't deserve to belong to the same species as Cole. Speaking of questionable males, how's it going with Reggie's father? I was surprised you let him babysit tonight."

Wade had shown up at Adrienne's door a few minutes past five, slightly out of breath and, apologetically, in need of a trip to the bathroom. He'd been on surveillance all afternoon, he'd explained. Too discreet to give details, he'd

simply said that most cases involved either cheating spouses
or fraudulent disability claims.

With his hair rumpled and his shirt open at the collar,
he'd been almost unbearably desirable. Also gratifyingly
cooperative. When Adrienne provided a schedule and other
directions, he'd promised to follow them to the letter.

She'd explained that Reggie was hyped up about the
overnight visit and might prove a handful. "I'll keep him
busy," Wade had promised.

Now Stacy awaited her response. "He's not what I expected," Adrienne said. "He's behaved like a gentleman. Although I am a little nervous about this overnight business."

"We'll be happy to watch Reggie anytime," Stacy offered.

"I'll be glad to return the favor with the triplets."

"I'm counting on it."

Adrienne's nurse, Eva, joined them to review the parting instructions while Adrienne went to write notes in the
computer. After everyone else left, she locked the office
and walked to the hospital.

Using a side entrance, Adrienne bypassed the lobby and
took the stairs to the third floor. During the four years since
she'd joined the staff, the medical center had completed its
remodeling from a community hospital to one specializing
in the treatment of fertility, pregnancies and other issues
affecting families. In the past year, an egg-donor program
and a men's fertility program had launched, as well.

Conferring with the charge nurse, Adrienne learned
there were half a dozen women in varying stages of labor.
She reviewed their charts and found labor progressing normally in all but one case, where the baby's heartbeat was
fluctuating. While the situation didn't appear dangerous
yet, a cesarean section might become necessary, and Adrienne ordered an operating room to be readied.

On the board, she saw that Dr. Paige Brennan was performing a C-section in another of the O.R.'s. "I thought she left early on Fridays," Adrienne commented. The obstetrician hadn't yet resumed a full-time schedule since the birth of her daughter nine months earlier.

"When she heard that her patient was upset and asking for her, Dr. Brennan insisted on coming in."

"I see." That was typical of how much Paige cared about her patients, Adrienne mused.

After she checked on each of the mothers, her next stop was the doctors' lounge, where she found the coffeepot half-full. This would be the first of many cups for the night. Adrienne doubted anyone ever completely adjusted to twelve-hour shifts four nights a week. Although the hospital provided sleeping rooms for on-call doctors, she rarely slept for more than a few hours.

While she was pouring, in breezed tall red-haired Paige. "Is there enough for me?" she asked in a soft Texas accent.

"You bet. This won't keep you awake?" None of the remaining patients were listed as Paige's, so presumably she'd be heading home.

"Caffeine doesn't bother me, and I like to unwind before facing my little tyrant. Oh, and the baby, too." Paige fixed herself a cup.

Adrienne laughed. "I can't imagine anyone but you describing Mike as little."

"Oh, he's a sweetie." Leaning on the counter, Paige took a swallow with obvious relish. "How're things going with Wade Hunter? Mike seems to like him."

Adrienne explained that he was babysitting tonight. "Reggie gets overexcited. I hope Wade can deal with that."

"As a cop, he should be good at conflict management and defusing tricky situations," Paige observed. "It's part of their training."

"With six-year-olds?"

"You have a point."

A quiver of uneasiness ran through Adrienne. It was nine o'clock, Reggie's bedtime. Should she call to say goodnight? She'd stopped doing that because it interrupted Mary Beth's evening and because her nephew insisted he was too grown up.

"You missed the divorce party," Paige remarked. "Zora threw quite a shindig."

"I heard."

"It's sad when people get divorced," the taller woman said. "In this case, though, anyone could've predicted Andrew wouldn't keep his pants on. Tigers don't change their stripes." She tossed her cup in the trash. "I'll brew more coffee before I go."

"Please don't bother. I can do it."

A pink-garbed hospital volunteer peeked through the open door. "Did somebody mention brewing coffee? That's my job."

"Renée! I didn't expect to see you tonight," Paige greeted the new arrival. "This is above and beyond the call of duty."

"Another volunteer called in sick, and I wasn't busy." In her sixties, with a rectangular face and graying hair, Renée Green was a fixture around the hospital. "I'm glad to be useful."

Although Adrienne had met the woman before, it took a moment to make the link between her and Paige, who greeted each other jovially. According to the hospital grapevine, Renée had recently found the son she'd long ago relinquished for adoption—none other than Paige's brother-in-law, Lock.

"If you're offering to make coffee, you have my gratitude," Adrienne told her.

"I'm here for another two hours. I'll make a fresh pot now and another before I go." As Paige departed, Renée went to the cabinet for the coffee and filter. "Did you see the darling cakes at the divorce party? I took a picture, if you're interested."

Out of courtesy, Adrienne agreed to see it. On Renée's phone the image showed two cakes, one white with a bride on top and one black with a groom. They were aiming toy pistols at each other.

"Well, there's a cheery image," Adrienne said.

"Being a widow, I've thought I might want to marry again, but this kind of thing makes me leery." After disposing of the dregs of the coffee, Renée rinsed the carafe. "Not that my boyfriend's the cheating type. His problem is being a control freak."

With Renée's openness about such personal matters, it was easy to see why she had a lot of friends. Adrienne couldn't imagine sharing her feelings that readily. "I can't bear having anyone try to control me."

"Neither can I." The older woman regarded her sympathetically. "Is something worrying you?"

"Why do you ask?"

Renée indicated the disposable cup Adrienne had squished in her hand. "I'd say that shows tension."

"It's my babysitting arrangements," she admitted.

"Wade's watching your nephew tonight, isn't he?" Renée said. "I haven't met him yet, but Lock speaks highly of him. I'm sure he'll do fine."

Were there any secrets in this hospital? Adrienne sighed. "I should call him before I get too busy."

"You'll feel better if you do." Renée finished preparing the pot, switched it on and went out.

Adrienne pressed Wade's number. He answered on the second ring, sounding out of breath. "Wade Hunter."

"It's Adrienne," she said. "Just making sure—"

"Reggie scraped his knee."

"How badly is he hurt?" she demanded. Although the

hospital didn't have an emergency room, the town's urgent-care center remained open until midnight.

"Nothing serious. I was about to patch him up." In the background, she heard voices. Reggie's, another boy's and a woman's, too.

"Where are you?"

"Playing catch in the street with some of the neighbors." Away from the phone, Wade said, "Don't touch it with your dirty hands. Let the blood wash the germs away."

Blood? Adrienne's stomach tightened. "Does he need stitches? He's up-to-date on his tetanus shots."

"I'll handle it, Doc," Wade said. "Where's the first-aid kit?"

"There's one in the downstairs bathroom and more supplies in the master bath."

Before she could say more, his voice cut in. "Oops, I'd better go. See you in the morning." He clicked off.

Adrienne stared at the phone as if it could transport her instantly home. Playing in the street? Running around at bedtime? And her little boy was injured. Instinct commanded her to rush to his aid. Surely she could slip out for half an hour.

Her phone rang. "Dr. Cavill," she answered.

It was the charge nurse, to report that the baby who'd concerned her earlier was showing signs of distress. The mom was being prepped for surgery.

Adrienne had to scrub in. She could only hope Wade was as competent as he seemed.

## Chapter Seven

On her way home Saturday morning, Adrienne started to head for Mary Beth's house before remembering that Reggie wasn't there. She felt a twinge of anxiety even though Wade had called last night after she finished the C-section.

Reggie's scrape had been cleaned and dressed, he'd assured her. Also, the neighbors they'd been playing with had invited them to go sailing this morning.

"We'll be out of your way while you're sleeping," he'd said.

It was on the tip of Adrienne's tongue to protest that she didn't know those particular neighbors very well. Bob and Lisa Rosen had moved in recently, and she wasn't sure they were careful sailors. All she said, however, was, "Be sure he wears a life jacket and sunscreen. Sunglasses, too."

"Check. And we'll see you before we go."

Sailing should be a good experience for Reggie, she told herself. Usually on weekends, Reggie either spent the morning with friends or had to tiptoe around the house while Adrienne dozed.

After parking in her garage, she entered via the utility room. The washing machine was humming. In her tired state, she stared at it before registering that Wade was running laundry. He must be doing the colored garments, since only the whites remained in a basket she'd left.

He'd set aside her delicate underwear. Cheeks heating,

Adrienne realized he'd sorted her bras and panties. She could hardly complain, since he'd done her a favor.

Glancing into the hazy mirror over the laundry sink, she shuddered at the reflected image. Bad enough to be several years older than this guy; no reason to show up with hair askew, makeup faded and dark circles under her eyes.

From her purse she took a brush and compact to perform some minor repairs. It might be silly, but she felt better.

She found Wade and Reggie in the den, on the floor reading a picture book. Below her nephew's shorts, a gauze bandage wrapped his knee. Adrienne resisted the urge to remove it and examine the injury.

Two sleeping bags were spread on the carpet, indicating they'd both slept down there last night. It must have been like a campout, she thought.

*When was the last time Reggie and I just had fun?* Even the best moments were always weighted by an awareness of her responsibilities.

"Did you guys eat breakfast?" Adrienne asked.

The faces that looked up at her bore a strong family resemblance, from the welcoming smiles to the raised eyebrows. "Toast and jam," Reggie replied.

"And milk," Wade added.

Although she usually served cereal and fruit, that sounded fine. "Thanks for starting the wash."

"I figured Reggie's old enough to learn how to run a load now that he's six."

In her perpetual rush to get chores out of the way, Adrienne hadn't considered that her nephew might be capable of doing laundry. "He helped you?" Oh, dear, had that included sorting her lingerie?

Perhaps guessing her concern, Wade said, "He measured the soap and set the water temperature."

Reggie's nose wrinkled. "Laundry stinks."

"Including yours, little buddy." Setting the book aside,

Wade gave him a nudge. Reggie shoved back. Pretend-punching each other in the shoulder led to a wrestling match on the floor.

Adrienne dodged their flailing limbs. "A pair of tough guys, huh?"

Wade let his son climb on top. "I win!" Reggie crowed.

"You're too strong for me," replied his father.

Bittersweet appreciation filled Adrienne. Since Vicki's death, she'd tried hard to be both mother and father. She'd done all right as mom, but she couldn't fill the role that came naturally to Wade.

*Oh, for heaven's sake, stop assuming you should be all things to all people.*

"I'll be in the kitchen," she said.

The place was spotless except for a glass in the sink. Adrienne recalled Wade saying he'd grown up in a chaotic home. Like her, he must have developed the habit of cleaning up as a way to restore order.

A minute later, Reggie came into the kitchen to give her a hug. She relished the feel of his small body pressed against hers. Little kids didn't stay little forever, and she cherished this stage.

"It's fun having a dad." He tilted his face up. "Thanks, Aunt Addie."

"For what?"

"My birthday surprise." Then, with a pride he rarely displayed for chores, he said, "I'm going to roll up my sleeping bag and take it upstairs."

"I'm impressed," Adrienne said. "You're acting so grown-up."

"Dad's teaching me." Beaming, the little boy scurried out.

Behind him, Wade ducked his head. "He's giving me more credit than I deserve."

"Regardless, you're a good influence." She took a container of yogurt out of the fridge.

Wade eyed it dubiously. "You consider that breakfast?"

"And you cook every morning?" she challenged.

"It's just that you're a doctor. I thought you'd be more…"

"Fussy?"

"Any answer to that would be wrong, so I'll pass." Turning a chair backward, he straddled it. "As you can see, we survived the night."

"You applied that bandage very neatly." She refrained from commenting that had her nephew gone to bed at his usual hour, he'd have avoided the injury altogether.

"But you were worried." Arms resting on the chair back, Wade added, "Any pointers about how I should handle things differently in future?"

She'd expected defensiveness, not a request for a critique. "You did great. First time out, you hit a home run."

"That's generous." He watched her aslant.

Not fully trusting her, Adrienne supposed. Well, she didn't fully trust him, either, but she was getting there.

"I'm beginning to understand how much Vicki cheated you and Reggie out of," she said. "You're so good with him, it's hard to imagine you being deprived of him all these years. And him of you."

His gaze was reflective. "When she broke things off, I had no idea she was pregnant. Eight and a half months later she phoned, hysterical, to say she was in labor. I showed up at the hospital, anxious to see my son. She had security kick me out. Claimed I was creating a disturbance."

"That sounds like my sister." Adrienne had also been on the receiving end of Vicki's mood swings. "She inherited bipolar disorder from our dad." He'd died of a drug overdose when she was twelve and Vicki was only seven.

"I should never have left Reggie to grow up in a situation like that." Wade shook his head. "They lived with your mom, right? What was she like?"

"Kindhearted, to a fault," Adrienne said. "Unfortunately, that meant she never stood up to my father or my sister about getting treatment. She died of cancer when Reggie was two. I'd just finished my residency at UCLA. I moved back here for his sake."

His expression softened. "No wonder you weren't happy about me mucking with your plans to adopt him."

"And—" She broke off.

"And you still aren't," he finished.

*Perceptive man.* "But you are good for him." Although hard to admit, it was true. "You're a world away from the other guys Vicki dated, and from what I expected."

"Glad to hear it."

What an idiot her sister had been to reject a guy like this. He stood head and shoulders above Vicki's other boyfriends as well as the jerks who'd let Adrienne down over the years. If she'd been in her sister's place... But she hadn't. And any attraction between them had to be kept at bay. Their first responsibility was to take care of their little boy, and that meant maintaining an emotional distance between her and this man.

Reggie scampered in. "I put everything away, Dad. Can you come next Friday night, too?"

Although she appreciated the help, Adrienne doubted they should start counting on him as a regular babysitter. "Wade might have to work."

"Yeah, although I'd like to, my hours are going to be irregular," he said.

That gave Reggie pause for about five seconds, before he blurted, "What about Thanksgiving? You could stay over that night. I'm tired of spending holidays with my sitter."

Adrienne gave a start. Although Thanksgiving was only two weeks off, she'd been so focused on planning Harper's wedding the following day that she'd assumed her arrangements were fine with her nephew.

Wade looked surprised. "You work on Thanksgiving?"

"My shift starts at eight. The trade-off is that I'm free on Christmas Eve and Christmas Day." Adrienne tried not to feel defensive.

"That sounds as bad as police work," Wade observed.

"So you'll stay over?" Reggie pressed.

Like it or not, Wade was part of their lives now. And Adrienne *had* been less than thrilled about the prospect of eating their holiday meal at a restaurant. "I suppose we could cook dinner here, the three of us."

"I'm afraid I already have a commitment," Wade said. "My father's counting on me."

Adrienne hoped her regret didn't show. "I understand."

"I have a grandpa?" Reggie gave a little hop. "I want to meet him."

Seeing the dismay in Wade's eyes, Adrienne recalled what he'd mentioned about his father's drinking. She waited for Wade to cough up an excuse. Instead, he sat down and took Reggie onto his lap.

"I'm not going to lie to you," he said. "My father isn't the grandpa type. I'm not sure he was ever the dad type, either. I used to take care of him as much as he took care of me."

"Is he sick?" the boy asked.

"In a way," Wade told him. "He has a disease called alcoholism. That means he sometimes acts like he loves drinking more than he loves his family. After my mother left, I did the laundry and fixed meals. Once in a while I had to sober him up in the morning so he could go to work. He's a good man at heart, but right now he isn't ready to be a grandfather."

Reggie pressed his lips together, thinking. Adrienne had discussed alcoholism with him before. Was he remembering a tipsy Vicki falling off a step stool the morning of his second birthday and bruising her hip? She'd cursed a blue streak, and they'd had to cancel the celebration while they took her to the emergency room.

"Okay," he said. "I'll wait till he's ready."

"Honestly, I'd rather spend Thanksgiving with you," Wade told him. "But I did promise."

"You should always keep a promise," the little boy responded firmly. "It hurts when people let you down."

"Yes, it does." She was glad Wade was reinforcing that value. "It's good to keep your word, even though it's our loss."

"My loss, too." Wade glanced at his watch. "We'd better be going."

After making sure Reggie had his key and arranging for Wade to phone if their sailing trip took longer than expected, Adrienne went to catch some sleep. Normally, she had trouble relaxing when Reg was with anyone other than his most relied-upon caretakers. Today, though, she wasn't as tense as she'd expected.

EVEN AFTER THE chill wind over the water was nothing but a memory and the abrasions on Wade's hands from helping to sail the boat began to heal, Saturday's outing lingered in his mind.

Reggie's energies were channeled as he cooperated with his new friends, eight-year-old Fred and his older sister, Marlys. They taught him the terminology of sailing, such as *boom* and *rudder, tacking* and *jibing,* and the directions: *aft, bow, port* and *starboard* instead of *back, front, left* and *right.* They also divided the task of scanning the waves for migrating whales, each child responsible for his or her own sector.

As for the parents, Bob and Lisa Rosen formed a smooth team. They spoke to each other and the children with respect, teaching while having fun. When a couple playful dolphins appeared, they shared in the youngsters' glee.

Being part of a family was fun. Wade regretted having to turn down Adrienne and Reggie's Thanksgiving invitation. He'd meant what he'd said about commitments, though. And if Daryl was alone on the holiday, he was likely to sink into depression and resume binge drinking.

As for Bruce, presumably his girlfriend was taking care of him. Besides, the old man must be steaming about Wade's new job, of which word had almost certainly reached him by now. Every time Wade considered phoning, his temper started to rise in anticipation of an argument. So far, he hadn't followed through.

Wade and Adrienne had scheduled their visit with the attorney for Thursday at 1:00 p.m. Wade didn't have to use his lunch hour; since he'd worked two nights this week to catch a man faking a disability claim, Mike let him take the afternoon off.

Once again, Adrienne beat him to the office. When she rose to shake hands, Wade noticed that her deep rose blouse brought out the color in her cheeks. "Nice outfit," he said.

"My favorite store was having a sale." She gazed up at him warmly. Her blond hair, tied back with a ribbon, gleamed with golden overtones.

"Did you do something different with your hair?"

"Highlights," she told him. "I figured I'd be too busy next week with the wedding."

"It makes you look younger."

She winced. "Uh…thanks."

"*Even* younger," he corrected, and she smiled. Age appeared to be a sensitive topic, although based on what Vicki had said when they were dating, he estimated her sister was a mere three years older than he was.

In Geoff's inner office, they explained that things were

going well. As before, the attorney recommended drafting a formal custody arrangement.

"I'm not ready for that," Wade said.

"Neither am I." Adrienne tapped the armrest of her chair. "But we could start to firm up a schedule."

That made sense. "I can pick up Reggie at his sitter's most Saturday mornings."

"That would be fine." She sounded relieved.

"I'm not sure where we'll go, though." Certainly not to Daryl's place.

"I'd be happy to draw up a list of activities," she said. "It doesn't have to be complicated. Kids like simple things, like visiting the beach or a playground."

"You seem to be moving toward a consensus rather nicely. I don't usually see such cooperation." Geoff cleared his throat. "However, I'd like to caution that you may both be averse to confrontation. If you're holding back, sooner or later you'll run into problems."

That was a startling insight. Wade's opinion of the man rose a notch.

"Despite my initial reservations, I'm comfortable with the way things are progressing," Adrienne said. "I don't believe either of us is afraid to be frank."

While Wade didn't want to read too much into the statement, he was glad his attempts at parenting met with her approval. Adrienne's good opinion meant a lot, both because of her experience with Reggie and because…

*Because I like her.* Nothing wrong with that.

The attorney reviewed options regarding custody. Shared custody seemed the most appropriate, when they were ready for that step. Even though, as the boy's surviving parent, Wade had a good chance of winning sole custody if he went for the jugular, the loser wouldn't only be Adrienne; it would also be Reggie.

"We could draw up a temporary visitation schedule

that allows for frequent ongoing contact with both of you," Geoff concluded. "Also, I should point out that there's a potential conflict of interest in having me represent both of you. I recommend hiring your own attorney."

"I'll take it under consideration." If things got messy, Wade wouldn't hesitate to do that.

Adrienne leaned forward. "I'd like for us to meet again after the first of the year, if that's okay with Wade. Let's see how our informal arrangements survive the holidays. By then we might be ready to put things down on paper."

"Survive the holidays—good way of putting it." In Wade's experience, family gatherings brought out the worst in people. They agreed that Wade would collect Reggie that Saturday morning. Then the lawyer escorted them out.

On the sidewalk, a sharp breeze blew beneath the overcast sky. "You in a hurry to get home?" Wade wasn't quite ready to give up her company yet.

"I have to run an errand for Harper." Adrienne crossed her arms against the chill. "The wedding's only a week away and we're behind."

Disappointment proved even keener than the cold wind. Couldn't the two of them have a conversation for once that didn't center on Reggie? Wade wasn't sure exactly what he sought, but being around her felt good.

Then an idea came to him. Shoving his hands into his jacket pockets, he said, "I'd like to pick your brain about something."

"What?" She tilted her head.

"Thanksgiving. I promised Dad I'd cook, but I have zero experience." Before she could suggest he look it up online, he added, "Internet sites often leave out crucial details."

"Like having to wash and chop ingredients *before* you start cooking," she said with a smile, and he grinned back. "I'm grateful for all those free sites, but they can be frustrating," she added, shifting so his body shielded her from the wind.

Wade didn't mind. He enjoyed protecting her. "You cold?" He reached out to enclose her hands in his and found them icy. "You're freezing!"

"And you're amazingly warm." She moved nearer, the lightly flowered scent of her hair tickling his nose.

When Wade leaned down and inhaled, he heard her breath catch. Only the rumble of a passing truck snapped him back to an awareness that they were standing in full public view. Reluctantly, he drew back.

"I'll tell you what." Adrienne shivered. "Let's meet at Kitchens, Cooks and Linens. That's where I'm headed, and it's a great place to discuss fixing Thanksgiving dinner."

"Great idea."

She provided an address on a side street near Fact Hunter. "Harper's been coveting their garden-themed linens and centerpieces, and they just went on sale."

"See you there."

She hurried away, crisp white skirt skimming her nicely rounded derriere. Missing their contact already, Wade strode to his car.

## Chapter Eight

Adrienne inhaled the scent of cinnamon as she entered the store and selected a rolling cart. One disadvantage of inheriting a furnished house was that she rarely had an excuse to indulge herself at Kitchens, Cooks and Linens. Except for picking up the occasional replacement item, she was confined by both her budget and her packed drawers to gazing longingly at the merchandise.

Shopping, even for someone else, was a treat. She'd volunteered to make the purchases because Harper had to work today and the selection might be depleted by evening.

After considering a Christmas theme for the wedding, Harper had instead chosen autumnal splendor. The colors not only worked well for her dress and bouquet but also tied into the colors of the garden. She'd fallen in love with a high-priced line of coordinated tablecloths, napkins and centerpieces.

The sale officially began tomorrow, but prices had been lowered a day early for subscribers to the store's mailing list. Because Adrienne had signed up, she'd received advance notice. Now she had two things to look forward to: she was not only shopping for her friend but also advising Wade, which might require additional purchases.

Strolling along an aisle, blissfully drinking in the luxurious sights and scents, she paused to stroke a velvety towel and examine an exquisite set of sheets. If she were getting married, she'd be tempted to denude the entire store.

"You're buying sheets for them?" The noise of other shoppers and carts had covered his approach.

Adrienne snatched an indulgent look at Wade. What a contrast between his muscular form and the delicate display of flowered duvets behind him. An image of his tanned body rumpling the bedding sneaked past her guard.

*Down, girl.*

"Actually, I'm dawdling," she said. "The section I want is over there."

"You really like this store, don't you?" Wade regarded her with interest.

"What do you mean?"

"You're wearing the same blissed-out expression that guys do at a car show." He studied her appreciatively. "It's good to see you enjoying something."

"I enjoy a lot of things." Now that he mentioned it, though, she didn't suppose that was true.

He strolled beside her, carrying a basket. "Maybe one of these days you can show me."

"One of these days." Adrienne quickened her pace as they neared the target area. To her relief, the tables and bins were nearly full. "Oh, great, these are perfect." She counted out the right number of cloths for their rented tables and scooped up matching items.

"That's quite a haul," Wade observed.

"I love this stuff." Adrienne had agreed to split the cost with her friend so she could keep some items. "So why did you volunteer to cook if you don't know how?"

Wade rearranged several items in her cart so they fit better. "I was worried about Dad. If he feels down about the holidays, his alcohol consumption will go up."

"I see." Adrienne picked up a set of crystal champagne flutes, admiring the way they sparkled even in the flat store lighting. "Speaking of alcohol, we were planning to use disposable champagne glasses, but these are beautiful. Can I resist?"

Wade laughed. "I've never seen anyone get this excited about glassware."

"Everything in this store turns me on." Embarrassed, she flicked him a cautious glance, then wished she hadn't, because the sight of his wry grin and square shoulders made her want to touch him. Firmly, she returned her thoughts to the glasses. "This is a great price. Do you need any? Oh, I didn't mean to be tactless."

"What's tactless about it?" he asked.

"I just meant if..." They'd agreed to be frank. "Do you have a problem with alcohol?"

He didn't appear offended. "I might be vulnerable under certain conditions. How about you?"

"More than one drink and I get sleepy. Since that's hardly my idea of fun, it's easy for me to drink in moderation." Adrienne was glad she didn't have to avoid the occasional glass of wine. "What do you mean by *certain conditions?*"

"I used to be able to drink as much as I liked with very little effect," Wade said. "Then one weekend I woke up in a strange woman's apartment with no memory of the night before. That scared me. I've seen too many mangled drunk drivers and their victims and too many criminals who lost control during a blackout."

"What did you do about it?" she asked.

"I quit completely. That's the only way to be certain I never lose control."

"That's admirable." Under pressure, even the most sincere resolve could falter, but Adrienne admired his determination. "Thanks for your honesty."

"It's one of my best qualities," he teased. "Now I have this other problem."

"What's that?"

"Thanksgiving," Wade reminded her. "I'm not sure where to start. For one thing, my father's kitchenware is strictly basic. He seems to consider more than one knife or pot a wild indulgence. Any idea what I'll need?"

An old saying came to mind: *When all else fails, read the directions.* "Let's check out the cookbook section."

They found shelves blooming with bright-covered cookbooks. After leafing through a few, they chose one that outlined step-by-step how to prepare a feast, including advance planning, a shopping list and recipes. Skimming it whetted Adrienne's appetite, both for the food itself and for filling the house with delicious scents. "You've inspired me to cook at home, too. To be on the safe side, I'd better buy my own copy."

"There's only one," Wade observed.

Scanning the rack confirmed what he'd said. Since he was the novice, she yielded it to him. "I can always order one on the internet." Besides, she'd already spent too much money today. "On second thought, I have a basic cookbook and I can find more recipes on the web."

"No argument from me." Wade held on to the book. "I'm a desperate man."

Following tips in the pages, he proceeded to buy a large disposable pan, a baster and two electronic meat thermometers to stick in different parts of the bird.

"Old-fashioned meat thermometers are cheaper." Adrienne had a couple of those in a drawer.

"But these beep."

"Seriously, that's a factor?"

Wade feigned a scowl. "Don't deprive a guy of his gadgets."

"Be that as it may," Adrienne said, "I doubt there's a high-tech way to stuff a turkey."

He blinked. "Stuff it?"

"Be sure to remove the giblets first."

"Uh…giblets?" Wade shifted his nearly full basket.

While it had been years since Adrienne had fixed a turkey, she hadn't forgotten *everything*. "They come in a little bag, hidden in the cavity. Once the turkey's defrosted, you pull them out and boil them for gravy."

"Defrosted?" Wade appeared increasingly uneasy.

"You can buy a fresh one, but those cost more." She folded her arms. "It's no big deal. You stick the frozen turkey inside that big pan and leave it in the fridge for a few days to thaw."

"All this for my dad, who doesn't much care what he eats as long as he gets to watch the football game." Wade shrugged. "Maybe I'm underestimating him. Besides, I should learn this stuff. I'll bring leftovers on Saturday so Reg sees that guys cook, too."

For a fellow who'd been an absentee dad, he was throwing himself into fatherhood full force, Adrienne reflected as they headed for the cashier. The odds of his leaving town were growing slimmer and slimmer, yet the observation failed to stir the usual twist of anxiety. He was good for Reg. And he was right about her—Adrienne didn't relax and have fun nearly often enough.

But she'd better be careful. People had a way of letting you down when you least expected it.

ON SATURDAY MORNING Wade picked up Reggie at his sitter's house as he'd arranged and took his son to the park. Pitching a ball around and taking turns on the slide worked the edge off their energy, so Wade was surprised when his son got cranky during lunch at a fast-food restaurant.

Nearby, a toddler pounded on her tray until her mother released her from the constraints and held her. At another booth, a family of five was sharing French fries and onion rings, laughing as they teased each other. "It's kind of noisy in here," Wade observed, wondering if that was the reason for his son's bad mood.

"It's not noisy," Reg grumped.

"Okay."

"This hamburger's too big." His son plopped it down on its wrapper.

"No law says you have to finish it."

"My teacher told us not to waste food," the little boy shot back. "There are children starving in Africa."

What was bothering him today? Wade recalled the saying that familiarity breeds contempt. Apparently their relationship had become familiar enough for Reg to argue with him. While that might be a good indication that he'd become part of the boy's world, he hoped he hadn't missed some important clue. "You can take the leftovers home."

"No. Hamburgers don't taste good in the microwave." Reg stared at his hands. "My fingers are greasy."

Wade finished a mouthful of his chicken sandwich. "You have my permission to go wash them."

"Come with me."

"Why? You're old enough." The place seemed safe, and Wade had a clear view of the restroom entrance.

"Mommy always went with me," Reg said.

Wade hesitated. "You mean your aunt?"

"No, my mommy."

Wade's impression was that Vicki had been an erratic mother at best. However, he saw no point in arguing. "One more bite and I'll be done."

Reggie sank down in his seat without replying. However, when Wade accompanied him, he washed his hands meekly.

The testy mood resurfaced after they reached home. The little boy ran ahead of Wade to the front door and, instead of using his key, punched the doorbell.

"Hey!" Wade ran to catch his wrist before he could do it again. "Your aunt's sleeping."

"She should get up." Reg's lower lip stuck out.

More puzzled than ever, Wade took the boy's key and let them inside. "Why?"

Instead of answering, his son ran upstairs. "Don't bother your aunt!" Wade shouted before realizing he'd no doubt awakened her by yelling. "Oh, hell."

A few minutes later, Adrienne descended the stairs, a soft green bathrobe bringing out the shade of her eyes while dark blond hair fell in disarray around her shoulders. Sleepy and invitingly tranquil despite the interruption, she held her nephew's hand.

Seeing Wade, she gave a start. "Oh, you're still here."

"Yep." Although that might be his cue to leave, he wasn't ready to. "He's been a real handful. I can't believe he's tired of our mornings together already."

Reg perched on one of the lower steps. "I'm not tired of them."

"Then what's wrong?" Adrienne sat beside him.

"Nothing." He sounded angry, though.

How was a parent supposed to react when a child refused to communicate? Wade clenched his hands in frustration. "I don't know what to do."

"When did this behavior start?" Adrienne probed.

Wade thought it over. "At the restaurant, he talked about his mother. I don't recall him doing that before."

"Other kids have their mommies," Reg muttered. "I miss her."

Drawing him close, Adrienne rested her cheek atop her nephew's head. Her gaze touched Wade's, and suddenly he understood. Despite Vicki's flaws, a mother was a mother, and seeing other kids with their happy families had hurt.

"We should go visit her today," Adrienne said. "It's been a few months. Too long."

"Can we?" Reg straightened.

"Sure."

"Can Daddy go with us?"

"If he's free," Adrienne said tactfully.

Although not thrilled by the prospect, Wade welcomed the fact that his son wanted to include him. *Guess I didn't screw up with him after all.*

"I'd be glad to join you." Wade had never been able to visit his own mother's grave, because she didn't have one. A few days after she'd died in the small-plane crash, her remains had been cremated and the ashes scattered at sea, as per her will. Because he'd been only sixteen, her adult stepson had taken care of the arrangements. While the idea of visiting a cemetery aroused painful recollections of loss, he understood why it was important for Reggie.

"You guys can pick flowers from the garden while I get ready," Adrienne said. "The calla lilies are in bloom, and I saw a few roses with buds opening." She gave details about the length of the stems and how to prepare them for the brass vase on the grave. They were to cut bunches for Reg's grandparents, too.

Eagerly, the little boy scrambled to his feet. "I'll cut them!"

"With your father's help."

"I'll fetch the clippers." Off he darted.

Wade was about to follow when Adrienne said, "Are you sure about this? You have no reason to mourn my sister."

"I mourn her for my son's sake," he responded truthfully. "And by the way, I'm impressed with your detective work about his mood."

Her mouth quirked. "Kids can be a mystery."

With her hair loose and her robe opening to reveal the lacy edge of her nightgown, she seemed different from her usual brisk self. Sensual, alluring and unguardedly female.

The kind of woman who belonged in a man's arms, being kissed at length.

*Wrong place, wrong time.* And, given the circumstances, wrong woman. "Thanks for inviting me." Wade strode in his son's wake.

The cemetery lay in the town's northeast section, near the freeway. On a Saturday afternoon, quite a few families were visiting loved ones, he noticed as Adrienne parked alongside the curving drive. They'd taken her car since it was larger.

"Mia's daddy is here," Reg announced as they got out. "So are Mommy and Grandma."

"And your grandfather, although you never knew him."

The graves were close together. A plaque marked Vicki's burial place, engraved with her name, birth and death dates and Dearly Loved Mother and Sister.

Solemnly, Reg positioned the flowers in the vases and added water from a bottle. It was peaceful here, Wade thought, gazing at the expanse of green.

So this was the final resting spot of the woman who'd turned his life upside down. Hard to believe all that exuberance, temperament and youth lay here quietly, forever.

"I wish she didn't die." Reggie wiped his eyes. "She used to laugh all the time. Except when she was sad."

"During her upbeat periods, she sparkled." The ache in Adrienne's voice reflected how much she, too, missed her sister. "Remember when she brought home a bunch of old Halloween costumes she'd spotted in somebody's trash? We couldn't believe people threw away perfectly good outfits."

"We wore them all day." Reggie smiled at the memory. "Even though Halloween was over."

"What kind of costumes?" The anecdote reminded Wade of how much fun Vicki had been while they were dating. She'd charmed him with her spontaneity, her ability to stay up all night without tiring and her enthusiasm in bed. He hadn't known until later that these might have been signs of the hyperactive phase of her condition.

"I was a panda," Reg announced.

"I took the witch costume," Adrienne recalled. "Vicki was a fairy princess. She looked beautiful."

"Take any pictures?" Wade would like to see those.

Reg scuffed his shoe on the grass. "Mommy threw them out."

"All of them?" What a bizarre thing to do. "Why?"

"She flew into a rage a few weeks later and deleted a whole bunch of photos from the computer and our backup." Regret and a hint of anger colored Adrienne's words. "Reg, I'm sorry. Your mom could be wonderful, but she suffered from an illness."

"Polar-bear disorder," he said earnestly.

About to correct him, Wade caught Adrienne's meaningful glance. They shared a moment of sorrow for what this boy had lost, and of joy for his dear innocence.

"Mia says angels watch over us," Reggie went on. "Do you think Mommy's an angel?"

Wade didn't answer. Even if he believed in such things, he hadn't forgotten Vicki's cruelty in separating him and Reg.

"Your mommy didn't deserve to suffer from a mental illness," Adrienne said. "If there's any justice, she's an angel now."

That was good enough for Wade. And as they left, Reggie began to hum "Teddy Bears' Picnic."

His son's good mood had been restored. And being there made Wade feel, just a little, as if he'd visited his own mother's grave, too.

THE DAY BEFORE Thanksgiving Wade left the office at 11:30 a.m. He intended to grab a quick bite and then stake out a position outside a motel where a client's husband was suspected of trysting with his girlfriend. According to the wife, her husband left his workplace for lunch about 1:00 p.m.

That gave him plenty of time to get into position. Better early than late.

He turned his key in the ignition. A clicking noise, then nothing. Cursing under his breath, Wade tried again. No response.

This morning, it had taken several attempts before the engine turned over. He'd attributed the difficulty to leaving the coupe outside in the early-morning cold.

Just what he needed: a dead battery. He'd have to wait for the auto club to send someone out.

He was about to call when Mike Aaron strode down the walkway. The tall sandy-haired man stopped by Wade's car. "Problem?"

"Dead battery. If you'll jump-start me, I'll be on my way." Wade explained where he was headed.

"You'll probably get stuck again."

No big deal. "Once the job's done, I'll have time to wait for the auto club."

Mike jiggled his keys. "I'll jump you, but please go straight to a mechanic. Places close early today and you could be without a car over the holiday. If lover boy has to wait till Monday, so be it."

"I'd rather do both. And I happen to know a good mechanic." If Daryl's garage stocked the right battery, he could fix it in a jiffy. If not, Wade would borrow his father's vehicle.

"You're resourceful. Good." With that, Mike went to move his silver sedan into the space beside the black coupe. "Nice wheels," he commented as he lifted the jumper cables from his trunk.

"Seemed like a great car when I had only myself and the occasional lady friend to transport." Wade opened his hood while Mike did the same with his car. "It seats two comfortably and three uncomfortably."

"Not too practical with a kid." His boss clamped a red cable end to the positive terminal on Wade's battery and the other end to his own battery. Then he checked to ensure he'd done it right. There was a slight risk of an explosion if anything got screwed up. Wade had seen that happen once in his high school parking lot, although luckily not to his car.

"Speaking of which, how's the fatherhood bit coming along?" Mike clamped a black cable end to the negative battery terminal on his sedan.

"Even more fun than I expected." Wade hadn't been prepared for Reggie's lovable nature. Nor for his aunt's tantalizing presence. "I'm glad he's old enough for us to do things together."

"That's a common misperception."

"What is?"

"That babies are boring."

"All they do is babble, cry all night and poop in their diapers, right?" Wade was only half joking.

Mike regarded him pityingly. "You missed the best part. There's nothing more fascinating than a baby."

With a smack of embarrassment, Wade recalled that he was talking to the father of an infant. "I meant the average kid," he amended. "I'm sure your daughter is a genius."

"That's a given." Mike broke into a fond smile. "They pull you into a new world."

"Yeah?" Wade had never seen this side of his boss.

"It's a real high, watching them." In his enthusiasm, Mike momentarily forgot his task. "Each week—each day—brings something new. Rolling over. Sitting up. Giggling as they play with you. Drinking out of a cup."

Giggling and drinking from a cup? An ironic remark

sprang to Wade's lips. Recalling how much he hated his grandfather's sarcasm, he restrained it.

"They're cunning little creatures," Mike added as he attached the other negative cable end to an unpainted bolt on the coupe. "They develop a startling resemblance to the woman you love, to you and maybe a few other relatives. They make you feel a part of generations in a way you never thought of before. Like, who had those eyes a hundred years ago? A thousand years? The DNA goes all the way back to the beginning."

Wade wasn't interested in Reggie's resemblance to Vicki. Now, if he had a baby with Adrienne, what a thrill it would be to see her knowing light green eyes staring up at him from a tiny face. Holding their baby in his arms, looking over and sharing Adrienne's joy—that would be special.

"We're set." Sliding behind his steering wheel, Mike switched on the sedan and let it idle. "See if that's enough juice."

Wade tried his ignition. After a brief grumble, it sprang into action. "Perfect."

Leaving his car on, Mike disconnected the cables. "Straight to the garage. I don't want this happening again."

"Me, either. Thanks."

Phil's Garage, where Daryl worked, was a couple blocks from the hospital. Wade was glad to see one of the bays empty and pulled into it.

The owner, Phil DiDonato, left the SUV he'd been working on and wiped his hands on a rag. "What's up, Wade?"

The guy had a good memory. Wade hadn't seen him since he used to bring his car there years ago. "I need a new battery. Is my dad around?"

The mechanic, a pleasant-faced guy in his mid-thirties, tugged on his blue coveralls. "Hasn't showed up yet."

It was nearly noon. "Is that normal?"

Phil ducked his head. "He's been pretty good since you came back to town, till today."

"What about before that?"

"It'd happen once, twice a week."

Wade hadn't realized his father was missing work. In fairness, Daryl might have been detained by a tenant's emergency. "When he comes in, is he hungover?"

Another pause, and then Phil said, "If he's not here by noon, he's not coming in."

That was even worse. Well, there was nothing Wade could do about it now. "Any chance of you replacing my battery? I realize you have extra work with my dad gone."

"It's a slow day. Let's see if I have the battery in stock."

Through his open window Wade inhaled the oddly reassuring scent of machine oil. He supposed he could grab a bite to eat at the hospital cafeteria while he waited. Then, double-checking the location of the Harbor Suites Motel in his phone, he realized it was right around the corner. That made sense. The place, which offered weekly suites as well as single rooms, probably catered to the families of hospital patients.

Along with a few marital cheaters.

Phil returned. "Yep, there's one left. I can switch that out for you inside of an hour."

"Great." Wade explained that he'd be back in an hour or two.

After retrieving his camera gear, he handed Phil the keys, provided his phone number and signed an estimate form. He also made sure his phone was on vibrate. Nothing like ruining the perfect shot because your phone drew your subject's attention.

He decided to skip lunch since he was behind schedule. En route to the motel, Wade wondered where his father was. At home, drinking?

Maybe once the job was done, he should swing by there.

But Daryl wasn't a child, and no one had appointed Wade his guardian.

He'd assumed his father was functioning, despite the occasional beer. Daryl had reinforced that impression, but a month of moderate restraint was apparently as much as he could bear.

*It isn't your responsibility.* Still, Wade hoped he could figure out a way to help his dad face up to his disease.

# Chapter Nine

The cheating husband, better dressed and groomed than in the photograph his wife had provided, showed up shortly after one, carrying a shiny gift bag, no doubt an attempt to pacify his girlfriend for his upcoming absence on the holiday. Wade caught excellent images of the man and the logo on the bag. That should help identify the purchase on the man's credit card.

He disappeared inside. Too bad. That meant no steamy embrace in public.

A second man, even more smartly dressed, strolled up to the room and tapped several times in a pattern. When he glanced around, Wade—lounging behind a tree—ducked back then captured the man's face through the branches.

The client was in for a shock. Maybe she'd feel some sympathy for a husband trapped by his fear of coming out about his sexual orientation. However, since he was betraying her trust and possibly putting her in medical jeopardy, Wade doubted it.

Half an hour later the second man stalked out, scowling. The husband emerged, still carrying the gift bag. Clearly, they'd quarreled. People who led double lives often destroyed both of them, in Wade's observation.

He walked to the garage, collected his refitted car and drove to the office. After writing the report, he forwarded it, with pictures, to Mike for review.

Time to go home and face what might be an unpleasant confrontation with Daryl. On the way Wade stopped at the Suncrest Market for some last-minute purchases, including a freshly baked apple pie.

Near the checkout counter a keepsake basket filled with yellow roses, orange lilies and red daisies caught his attention. Adrienne would love those. However, Wade doubted they'd stay fresh until Saturday, when he was scheduled to pick up Reggie. Also, she'd have lots of flowers left from Friday's wedding.

In the line, carts were piled high with turkeys, yams, stuffing mix and other goodies. The shoppers must be expecting large crowds for their meals, or else love leftovers. Or both.

Once again Wade was on the outside looking in. After his mother left, he used to take walks on Thanksgiving to escape the gloomy apartment. Delicious cooking smells would fill the air. Later, in December, Christmas trees twinkled through the front windows while colored lights and lawn displays turned the neighborhood into a fantasyland. His sense of longing had cut like a razor blade.

Finally, it was his turn to unload his groceries. He was buying a lot of food for two people, he reflected. Overcompensating, no doubt.

At Daryl's apartment the sour smell of beer struck him in the doorway. Carrying the groceries to the kitchen, Wade passed his father, who was sprawled on the couch watching a reality show.

*You've been in denial.* His father might have limited his drinking for a few weeks rather than show weakness in front of Wade. Now he'd returned to his normal habits. If the man didn't get a grip, he'd soon find himself jobless and possibly homeless, as well.

While putting the groceries away, Wade debated how

to proceed. Or whether to say anything, since that risked a fight unlikely to produce a resolution.

"You buy any beer?" Daryl called.

"Didn't realize you were out of it." Since he disliked yelling from one room to another, Wade walked to where he could see his father. "Phil replaced my battery today."

"Yeah?"

"I was surprised you weren't there."

"My drinking is my business." So much for the cautious approach; his father had leaped right to the main point.

"It's Phil's business, too," Wade observed testily. "He's a nice guy, but if the work piles up, sooner or later he'll hire another mechanic."

"He can take that lousy job and shove it." Daryl hefted his can, glared at it for daring to be empty and crumpled it. "I deserve a real job, the kind I'm trained for. You tell Mike Aaron he oughta hire me."

Wade tried not to show his dismay. "Have you applied?"

"Sent him a résumé. Never got a response," Daryl retorted. "I'm a seasoned hand and I'd bring in clients. My father founded the place, in case he's forgotten."

If Wade's father believed he was in any shape to take on a job requiring dependability and discretion, he'd lost touch with reality. Most likely, it was the alcohol speaking.

A knock on the door provided a welcome interruption. A tenant's oven was on the fritz. Daryl went to inspect it, muttering that he'd have to pay double for a repairman on the eve of a holiday.

In the kitchen, where Wade resumed stowing his purchases, he mulled Daryl's idea of working at Fact Hunter. With luck, his father would drop the subject. Wade hoped so, because there was no way Mike Aaron would hire him.

Not unless his father made a lot of changes. And that wouldn't happen overnight.

By LATE AFTERNOON on Thanksgiving Day, Adrienne's house smelled of sausage-and-sage stuffing. She had fresh yams ready to put in the microwave and a salad in the refrigerator. A pumpkin pie sat on a side counter.

The problem was the turkey. She'd bought it two days ago, assuming it would thaw. This morning, she'd discovered the inside still frozen, the packet of giblets too solidly attached for removal. She'd bathed it in cold water, changing the water every half hour, and had finally brought it to a passable level.

She hoped to stuff it quickly, but she hadn't counted on Reggie. "This is what my dad's doing today, right?" he asked.

"Yes, he is." Adrienne wished they could share this task. It would be fun cooking together. Well, maybe another day.

"Let me do it, too. Please!"

Despite running late, she agreed. Her nephew washed his hands—thank goodness—and then, without waiting for instructions, began shoving handfuls of stuffing from the bowl into the bird.

"Wait!"

"Why?" he demanded.

"We haven't removed the giblets." Explaining that those had to be cooked separately, she emptied the turkey and they started over.

It was two o'clock when the bird—stuffed, tied and giblet-free—went into the oven. With an estimated four-hour cooking time plus an hour of standing before carving, it would be a close race to eat dinner before they left for Mary Beth's house at seven-thirty.

Adrienne set to cleaning the kitchen. Through the window, she saw that the predicted rain had begun to fall.

Despite her efforts to relax, she kept reviewing the wedding arrangements. She'd told the rental service to leave the tables and chairs for forty guests folded under the patio cover. Harper and Peter would arrive at 9:00 a.m. tomorrow to set them up and hold a quick walk-through of the ceremony. But if the lawn didn't dry off, they'd have to activate their emergency backup plan and move everything indoors.

*What was I thinking when I offered to a host a wedding?* That it would be a lot of fun, Adrienne recalled. And perhaps it still would be.

In the family room, she collapsed into an upholstered chair. With a long night ahead, she could use a nap.

The phone rang.

*Please don't let that be Labor and Delivery.* Today of all days, she wasn't prepared for the charge nurse to summon her early.

Grimly, Adrienne fumbled in her pocket and drew out the phone.

THANKS TO THE SPICES Wade had infused the previous day following the instructions in the cookbook, the turkey emerged from the oven at three o'clock deliciously browned and smelling irresistible. Daryl followed his nose into the kitchen. "Let's eat!"

"It has to sit for an hour before I carve it." Wade planned to follow a video, since turkey carving was no simple matter.

"Who invented that rule?" his father grumbled.

"The salad's ready, if you're hungry."

"Rabbit food." Daryl returned to the couch and the stash of beer he'd replenished last night. Wade resented that his father wasn't even trying to moderate his drinking. The main point of cooking this meal and missing the holiday with Reggie had been to prevent a binge like this. Not that his father had agreed to that premise, but he could expend a little more effort to be sociable.

In Wade's pocket the phone vibrated. It was Adrienne, he saw with a lift of spirits. "What's up?"

"They need me at work early." She sounded near tears.

"On a holiday?" He bristled on her behalf.

"I'm sure the moms in labor would wait if they could," she replied. "The problem is that a lot of doctors are out of town, and the obstetrician on duty can't handle everything."

"You have to go in right away?" He wondered if he dared suggest she drop Reggie off there. Given Daryl's unstable mood, that was a dicey proposition.

"I discussed the situation with Zack Sargent—the OB who has this shift—and he can hold the fort alone for another hour or so," she said. "But my turkey won't be done until six. Also, I reached Mary Beth and honestly, I could tell it's a major imposition to bring Reggie early. She wasn't thrilled about babysitting tonight in the first place."

"Tell her she's relieved of duty. I'll be over in…" Wade made a quick mental calculation. "Give me half an hour— forty-five minutes max."

"What about your dinner?" she asked.

"Turkey's out of the oven and my sweet-potato casserole's done." He'd break the rules and carve some meat for Daryl. "What else should I bring?"

They compared notes. She had salad and pumpkin pie and didn't mind saving her yams to eat another day. "I can whip up the mashed potatoes from a box. What about gravy?"

That had to be fixed with drippings from the bird. Although he'd suctioned them into a pan, he hadn't added seasoning or thickening yet. "I'll bring the liquid with me. Shouldn't take long."

"You don't mind?" she asked. "You'll need to pull my turkey out of the oven when it's done."

"No problem." There'd be a huge supply of leftovers, but they could always freeze those.

"Reggie will be thrilled," Adrienne said. "You're a saint."

"No one ever called me that before." The compliment warmed Wade. "I'll fix a plate for my father before I go."

"I'm sorry about that." Sympathy quivered in her voice. "That poor man, alone on Thanksgiving."

"He'll hardly notice I'm gone," Wade assured her, bitterness creeping into his voice. "He can watch football and swill beer in peace."

Too late he realized he should have skipped the sarcasm. From the doorway, Daryl glared at him.

"See you in a bit," Wade said. "Gotta go."

"Thank you a thousand times."

"I'm glad someone appreciates me." After clicking off, Wade faced his father. "I'm sorry. That was rude."

"Doesn't change the fact that my own son disrespects me."

Having apologized once, Wade didn't intend to do it again. "Guess I learned my bad manners from Grandpa."

His father's anger, always easily provoked, wasn't about to fade. Instead, Daryl fixed on another cause for complaint. "You have no intention of putting in a good word with Mike Aaron, do you?"

*Let's not get into that now.* "It isn't my place to order my boss around."

"You think I'm unfit for your job." His hands flexing, Daryl braced for a fight.

Since it seemed impossible to avoid an argument, Wade told the truth. "As long as you keep drinking, I can't recommend you."

"You owe me!" The words burst out.

"Owe you for what, exactly?"

"For how hard I've worked," his father snapped. "All the sacrifices I've made."

Wade's patience evaporated. "You're not the only one who made sacrifices. I grew up rescuing you from bars when you were too drunk to drive, doing your laundry, fixing your meals, getting you up and into the shower when you were hungover so you wouldn't lose your job. Dad, I'll help you fight this thing if you'll let me, but I refuse to pretend everything's fine. It isn't."

"Get out!" Rage contorted Daryl's face. "Take your damn clothes and clear out of my apartment."

"Fine." Wade hadn't meant to cause a breach, and he'd have preferred to move out on good terms. But he had a place to stay tonight, and he'd rent a place after that.

He threw his possessions together and carried them to the car. On his return he found Daryl in the kitchen, eating stuffing and yams piled on a plate. Quickly, Wade cut off both turkey legs and thighs and left half the apple pie, as well.

He poured the drippings into a jar, put the turkey and pan into a large shopping bag and scraped the rest of the yams into a disposable container. He'd already spread a couple large towels in the trunk in case anything spilled. "I'll let you know when I'm settled."

"Whatever." His father stared down at his plate.

Wade replaced the spare key on the Peg-Board and took the remaining pie. By some miracle, he reached his car without dropping anything. Reviewing the blowup en route to Adrienne's, he conceded that he shouldn't have insulted his father, but he'd apologized. Now they were alienated, just like him and Grandpa.

Not setting a very good example of family togetherness for Reggie, was he?

On Adrienne's street, her house glowed with welcome. The fading November sunlight played lovingly over the cream-and-blue paint and the cheerful plantings. The orange-and-violet birdlike flowers rose on long stems from the bird-of-paradise plant while his yellow miniature rose added cheer to the low-growing border.

She'd planted it. Wade was touched.

He opened his trunk and was deciding what to take inside when Reggie ran out. "Daddy!"

"Hey, sport." Crouching, Wade braced for impact.

After the hug, the little boy helped cart in the food. Bringing his suitcase as well as the turkey, Wade inhaled pleasurably as he stepped into the house. Dinner smelled even better here than at the apartment.

In the kitchen, Adrienne grinned at him, brushing back a strand of blond hair that had escaped her clip. She'd set three places in the breakfast nook with fine china and silverware.

"I figured it would be cozier to eat in here than the dining room," she explained. Beneath her apron she wore navy slacks and a dark pink blouse. Perhaps the layers she had on or the heat from cooking accounted for the blush on her cheeks.

With time running short, they divided the tasks, Adrienne making gravy and Wade—watching the video— carving the bird. Reggie disappeared, only to pop in and announce, "I put Dad's suitcase in Mom's old room."

*The room where Vicki used to sleep.* When Adrienne's forehead puckered, Wade feared she might reprimand the boy, who'd meant well. "That'll keep my stuff out of the way when people arrive early tomorrow," he said. "There must be a lot of preparations still to make."

Adrienne sighed. "Yes. Good thinking, Reggie." She closed her eyes wearily.

"You okay?" If Wade's hands hadn't been occupied with carving, he'd have reached for her.

"After I called you, Harper phoned to say their deejay is down with the flu. I'll have to commandeer one of the guests to run the music."

"I can do that." Wade didn't mean to intrude, since he hadn't been invited to the wedding. "If it's not presuming too much."

"Presuming? You're doing us a favor."

"Yay!" Reggie danced around the kitchen. "Dad's the music man."

Since he'd be sticking around until tomorrow evening, Wade put in, "Why don't I stay over Friday night? I'm spending Saturday with Reggie anyway."

"That'll give Mary Beth a longer break. She could use one." Adrienne said. "Thank you. I seem to be saying that a lot, don't I?"

"And I never get tired of hearing it."

As for being temporarily homeless, Wade decided to save that news. He'd choose a moment when Reggie wasn't around to urge that Daddy move in.

Tempting as the idea was, putting pressure on Adrienne might destroy this tentative bond between them. For now, Wade was simply glad to be in a real home for the holiday.

## Chapter Ten

On Thursday night everything went well in Labor and Delivery. Babies were born quickly, the influx of laboring moms diminished and although Zack had a wife and two daughters at home, he stayed late to perform a C-section. "We had our holiday dinner last night," he explained.

Adrienne managed to catch four hours' sleep. Meanwhile, according to the weather report, the rain had not only passed out to sea but been replaced by a mild Santa Ana condition. That meant drying winds and warm temperatures, perfect for the wedding.

When Reggie announced that he'd put Wade's belongings in Vicki's room, Adrienne had nearly ordered him to move them to her old bedroom, which she'd vacated for the master suite. However, she was even less comfortable with the notion of the virile male sleeping in her bed than in her sister's.

In the morning, Wade more than earned his keep. He helped arrange chairs and tables and set up the rented sound system. He tied yellow and red balloons to the front porch and posted neatly printed signs directing guests into the yard through an inconspicuous side gate.

Instead of growing impatient with having Reggie underfoot, Wade seized every opportunity to teach—how to hold a hammer and how to lift rather than drag the chairs. The boy complied willingly.

Adrienne retreated to the kitchen, where she found Peter's mother, Kerry, a retired teacher, setting out plastic champagne glasses. "I'll handle the food when the caterer arrives," Kerry said. "I'm sure you and our new daughter-in-law have plenty of other things to do."

"I appreciate that."

"I prefer keeping busy." The older woman brushed at her misty eyes. "Now shoo!"

With Stacy and Cole weaving chrysanthemums through the wedding arch and Harper's brother, Jake, handling other tasks, Adrienne took a deep breath. *Slow down. Everything's under control.*

She and Harper shepherded Mia upstairs to dress. The little girl twirled about in the master bedroom, her green-and-gold dress bringing out the green of her eyes. "After today Peter's my daddy for real!" she cried. "Isn't he, Mommy?"

"Yes, he is." Tall and elegant in her scarf-hemmed cocktail dress, its colors coordinated with her daughter's, Harper met Adrienne's gaze over Mia's head. "I'm glad the surrogate isn't due to deliver the twins until June. Mia needs this time with her new father and me."

"Can I go downstairs now?" her daughter begged.

Harper applied a brush to an errant tuft of the girl's hair. "Now you're ready. Help Grandma Kerry, okay? No playing in the yard."

"Okay, Mommy." Off she scampered.

"I'm so happy you've found love again." Adrienne slipped on her own dress, which had a subtle autumn-leaf design.

"Thanks." Harper took a seat at the vanity. "I just can't help thinking about the people who aren't here. Especially Vicki."

"My sister would be thrilled for you," Adrienne said. "But I miss her, too."

"And my parents." Harper adjusted a gauzy hat atop her smooth honey-colored hair.

"I'm sure they're here in spirit." Adrienne came over to place the hat at a more flattering angle.

"Perfect!" Harper grinned. "Now, what's the deal with Wade?"

"What about him?" To forestall further questions, Adrienne asked, "You don't mind him being here, do you?"

"Heck, no." In the mirror, her friend's eyes widened. "A volunteer deejay? What a blessing. But I wondered... I mean, he's practically living in your house."

"Only for a few days. We had a babysitting emergency last night." With a twinge, Adrienne recalled Reggie's invitation to his dad to share their home. Having him live there *would* be convenient. And dangerous. She wasn't even sure Wade wanted to live with them, she reminded herself.

"You have a babysitting emergency practically every week," Harper teased as she applied makeup. "Your schedule is murder."

"I'm used to it." That wasn't entirely true. Last night when the charge nurse had called, Adrienne had come close to having a meltdown.

A knock drew her to the door. She admitted the photographer, a bearded young man who positioned the two of them for a few shots. With the door open, Adrienne could hear people arriving downstairs.

The show was about to begin.

OVER THE YEARS, Wade had attended his share of weddings, most involving fellow officers. He'd never taken part in one, though. While he'd formed friendships at work and hung out with other guys, he'd never grown close enough to be invited as a groomsman. Hadn't given it a moment's thought, either.

Today, with dozens of people around, he was glad to

have a specific task. Even though he recognized some of the guests, Wade couldn't keep track of everyone or how they were connected. He pretended to be occupied with the sound system, although all he'd had to do so far was pop in the CD labeled As Guests Arrive, which featured Vivaldi, Bach and other baroque composers.

"Excellent choice of music." A russet-haired man joined him on the patio. "You're the deejay, I take it."

"Wade Hunter." Extending his hand, he found the newcomer's grip firm and his gaze intense.

"Owen Tartikoff," the man said. "Listen, at some point after the ceremony, my wife and I plan to sing a few songs for the happy couple. Hope that doesn't mess up your playlist."

"No problem." Following Owen's gaze, Wade saw a guitar case leaning against the house. "Yours, I presume?"

"It isn't in the way, is it?" the man asked.

"Not at all."

"I'll let you know when we're ready." After clapping Wade on the shoulder, Owen strode off. Others spoke to him deferentially.

Adrienne glided up beside Wade. "What was that about?"

"He and his wife are going to sing later," he told her. "Hope that's okay."

She gave him a wry grin. "Owen's the head of the fertility program and has a world-class reputation."

"But can he sing?" That seemed the relevant point to Wade.

"Beautifully," she said. "So can his wife, Bailey." With that, Adrienne moved off, greeting new arrivals and steering Reggie to his seat.

Wade checked his watch. Nearly 3:00 p.m., the designated start time. Sunlight bathed the flower-filled arbor where the groom waited between his father and the minister.

At a prearranged signal, Wade put on the CD marked Ceremony and sat back.

As HARD AS Adrienne tried to push the past from her thoughts, the ghosts of former times—both happy and bittersweet—overlay the ceremony. This was the yard where she and Vicki used to play as children, staging pretend weddings and taking turns at being the bride. Until this moment, she'd almost forgotten that.

She welcomed the distraction as Mia skipped down the aisle, waving her bouquet of autumn flowers. At the end, with an audible "Oops!" she slowed her pace to match the wedding march. Her new stepfather barely smothered his laughter.

Then the ghosts closed in again as Harper, shining with joy on her brother's arm, strolled down the aisle, her dress flowing like a fall breeze and her hat tilted jauntily. For a moment, Adrienne was back in the chapel where Harper had married Sean. How happy she'd looked in her white gown, dewy and young, without the wisdom and sorrows of the years to shade her gaze.

Adrienne's eyes smarted. Were the tears for Vicki, who ought to be here? For herself, who'd set aside her childish dream of finding true love? Or because a wedding reminded her of all the hopes that might or might not come true?

*Enjoy this moment. It's the only thing that's real.*

Wade was real, too. Despite the urge to glance at him, Adrienne didn't dare. Her friends would notice. If Harper was any indication, they were already gossiping.

At the altar, Harper's brother presented her to the groom. The bride handed her bouquet to Mia, who wrapped her arms around both bunches of flowers and lifted them to her nose.

Then the minister began the ceremony.

AFTER THE VOWS were exchanged and the guests had cheered for the newlyweds, it was time to take photos and set up for dinner. Under Adrienne's direction, everyone picked up his or her chair and carried it to a table.

Wade assisted the groom's mother in arranging the buffet on the patio. "You're a good sport," Adrienne told him, hurrying past with a large catering pan.

"I'm enjoying this." And, surprisingly, he meant that.

Reggie scampered toward them. "Are they going to open the gifts now?" A small table held wrapped packages.

"No, they'll do that later at home." Adrienne stopped to pat her nephew's cheek. "You were very patient during the ceremony."

Reggie's gaze shifted to Wade. Realizing his son craved his approval, too, he said, "You acted like a grown-up." Since the boy brimmed with energy, he added, "It's your job to play host for the other children." There weren't many, since only those of school age had been invited.

Reggie frowned. "Like how?"

"See if any of them need to use the bathroom," Adrienne suggested.

"Okay!"

"And make sure they wipe their feet before they go inside," Wade cautioned.

"Sure, Dad." He darted off.

Adrienne's attention shifted to Wade. "There's no formal seating. Grab a plate, find a place and get comfortable."

"What about the dance music?" He didn't intend to neglect his duties.

"We'll let you know when it's time."

He gave a mock salute. "You're in charge."

"If you call me ma'am, I'll kick you."

"I'd prefer a spanking." He waggled his eyebrows.

Adrienne laughed. "Don't let anyone hear you. They're spreading enough rumors about us already."

That was interesting information. "Will I need to fight a duel to defend your honor?" Wade asked.

"I'm pretty good at defending my own honor," she returned lightly.

He grinned. "I'm sure you are."

Seeing this playful side of her showed what a mischievous spirit she must have had as a child. Her parents' and sister's deaths had changed her.

Wade hoped to lighten her mood more often.

ADRIENNE WOULD HAVE liked to sit near Wade. Instead, she felt obligated to join a table across the lawn to avoid inspiring more chatter.

The group of pregnant women surrounding Wade included Vanessa Ayres—Peter and Harper's surrogate. Then there was Stacy, her triplets growing larger by the day, and Una Barker, whose twins were due in January. She'd become pregnant the same month as Stacy, with Stacy's donated eggs, and their children would be half siblings.

They were all very discreet, with their husbands present. But Wade certainly seemed to take an interest. At Una's urging, he leaned forward and touched her large belly, perhaps to feel the babies moving.

It was ridiculous to fret. Given how much Wade enjoyed being around Reggie, it seemed natural for him to take an interest in babies.

*But there won't be any of those for me.*

Pain arrowed through Adrienne for the children she'd never have, the future that had been stolen from her by a tragic accident. She'd believed that she'd put regret and sorrow behind her long ago and channeled her love of children into her specialty in obstetrics. And it had worked, to a point.

Initially, as a result of her family's issues, she'd planned to become a psychiatrist. But delivering her first baby had filled Adrienne with joy. Who needed alcohol or drugs when she could achieve such a high from bringing newborns into the world?

In other aspects of her practice, her experiences gave her empathy for patients. When they suffered disappointments, she understood. And each time she helped a couple get pregnant, she shared in their triumph, becoming part of a cycle that had otherwise shut her out. Plus, she had Reggie to love.

*I have a lot to be grateful for.* Despite his legal right to claim custody, Wade was willing to work with her in Reggie's best interests, and she didn't begrudge him the chance to have children someday with another woman. Yet despite her determination not to dwell on matters beyond her control, it hurt to see the light in his face as Una's belly rippled.

To her embarrassment, Adrienne realized she was staring at him. So was the woman beside her, Keely Randolph, the R.N. who assisted Paige. The heavyset older woman was scowling.

"The way that fellow's drooling, those husbands better keep a close watch on their wives," Keely said in her nasal voice.

"What do you mean?" Adrienne didn't think he had any predatory intentions toward the wives at his table.

"Some fellas get the hots for ladies with a bun in the oven," the nurse observed dourly. "And what those hormones do to some women's libidos, well, it's shameful." She shook her graying black hair.

Adrienne doubted any of the mothers-to-be was about to drag Wade under the table. The absurd statement had the welcome effect of banishing her dark thoughts.

So did the toasts that followed. Peter's father talked about the difficulties of the past and how grateful he and his wife were that their widowed son had found such a wonderful woman. Then Jake, who'd flown in from New Mexico to be with his sister, spoke about their losses and the blessing of her new love with Peter.

Adrienne circulated, refilling champagne glasses for others while taking only a few sips from her own glass. Wade sprang up to pour apple juice for the kids and for himself. Then, at a signal from Peter, he returned to the CD player.

Time for the bride and groom to circle the dance floor set up adjacent to the vegetable garden. This ought to keep Wade busy and out from under the table, Adrienne thought good-humoredly, and moved to collect empty plates.

ALTHOUGH HE HADN'T selected the music, Wade liked the choices, an appealing mix of beats, artists and styles. The guests clearly enjoyed the playlist as well, laughing as they danced. Reggie got into the act, taking turns with Mia and Fiona, who also partnered with their fathers.

For a change of pace, Mike and Paige performed a steamy tango—Wade would never have believed his boss capable of such artistry on the dance floor—after which Owen Tartikoff claimed Paige for a showy cha-cha. Owen's wife apparently didn't mind; a short, lively woman, Bailey applauded with enthusiasm.

All the while, Wade tracked Adrienne's movements. She didn't dance with anyone, always busy with her hands full as if to discourage an invitation. She kept a watchful eye on her nephew, as well.

Talking with the mothers-to-be during the meal had increased Wade's appreciation for what Adrienne did. Those long nights were spent bringing newborns into the world, reassuring their parents and stepping in with lifesaving surgery when needed. Amazingly, she also ran her home smoothly. Rather than growing up in turmoil, Reggie thrived in an atmosphere of structure combined with love.

When Wade had first met Adrienne, he'd scarcely noticed how attractive she was, especially compared to her sister's more striking blond looks. Now she outshone all the other women at the wedding, including the bride. With her gift for compassion and her natural beauty, she'd no doubt have married and had children by now if not for her responsibilities.

As Wade watched her and the groom's mother bring out the wedding cake and champagne, he pictured Adrienne growing round with pregnancy. Longing stabbed him to be the man who fathered that new life.

*Hold on there.*

Wade was in no shape financially to take on a wife and kids, even if Adrienne didn't exhibit an understandable level of wariness around him. Also, they had to be cautious, given their potential for conflict over Reggie and the fact that both came from dysfunctional families.

Still, any guy who came calling on Adrienne had better treat her right. Otherwise, he'd have to answer to Wade.

A song ended, and she headed toward him. Recalled to duty, he stopped the CD player so she could announce the cake cutting.

After she finished, Wade switched off the sound before addressing her. "You're doing a great job. I hope people appreciate your hard work."

With a trace of weariness, Adrienne murmured, "I don't expect praise. I'm doing this for my friend."

"You should take a compliment when it's offered. You deserve it." The booming voice belonged to Owen, who'd strolled up and wrapped an arm around her waist.

Feeling an urge to protect his territory, Wade narrowed his eyes. But the russet-haired fertility specialist didn't appear to be flirting. He was merely offering support in his aggressive way.

"Thanks." Tossing out the word at both of them, Adrienne escaped.

"When everyone settles down with their cake, my wife and I will be singing our special tribute," Owen informed Wade, and strolled off.

A short while later the doctor returned with his cheerful wife. Leaning against the table, he rested one foot on a chair and tuned the guitar. Wade positioned the microphone between the two of them.

After a few chords to summon everyone's attention, the couple began to sing. They chose songs that Wade recognized from the musical *Carousel:* "If I Loved You" and "When I Marry Mr. Snow."

Bailey's pure alto and her husband's smooth baritone soared into the late afternoon, transporting their listeners. Eyes half-closed, Wade listened with pleasure. These two obviously loved their music, as well as each other.

Reggie and a couple little girls moved to the front of the crowd. Their enraptured expressions made them the ideal audience.

An ovation rewarded the end of each song. Cries of "More!" rang out from the guests.

To Wade's surprise, Reggie cut off the concert by running up to the tall, commanding doctor. "It's my dad's turn now," he said.

"Your dad?" Owen asked.

Across the group, Wade's startled gaze met Adrienne's. She spread her hands in amusement, as if to ask how he could resist his son.

"I'm only here to play recordings," Wade said.

Owen swung toward him, mouth open for a millisecond as he registered that the deejay was Reggie's father. "You

should sing, by all means. Don't disappoint the little boy."
He handed over the guitar.

*Oh, great.* Wade, who rarely sang for others, was about
to make his debut in front of a crowd. Not that they were
likely to pelt him with wedding cake if he sang off-key, but
he'd hate to embarrass Adrienne.

He wished he'd rehearsed something appropriate. Then
he got an idea.

# Chapter Eleven

Adrienne hadn't meant to leave Wade in an awkward position. As deejay, he'd unintentionally taken center stage. And while he had a bewitching tenor voice, his guarded personality put him at a disadvantage next to Owen.

Yet he exuded quiet confidence as he accepted the instrument and checked the tuning. Then he waved to Reggie and the little girls to join him.

His son plopped happily at his feet, while Mia and Fiona gathered around them. When Wade played the first notes of "Teddy Bears' Picnic," the children joined in singing gleefully. If the notes were a bit ragged and the lyrics occasionally strayed, the result was to add even more charm.

He didn't need to show off, because, Adrienne could see, he wasn't trying to impress anyone. Instead, Wade blended his voice with the children's in the lighthearted song.

As dusk closed in, the patio lights created a glowing spotlight on the small group. What a magical moment, and what a tender, kindhearted father.

When they finished, a moment of silence yielded to a swell of applause. Adrienne saw a couple people wiping their eyes.

Wade consulted with the children before launching into the song "Edelweiss" from *The Sound of Music*. Again the kids sang with him, and one by one, other voices blended in.

All the sorrows the house had seen faded before the joy

of the shared experience. How astonishing that music could sweep away the regrets and make everything fresh again.

*Not just the music. Wade did this.*

Afterward, the children took their bows. Although Reggie asked for more songs, Fiona shook her head and Mia followed suit. "You guys were great," Wade said, adding for his son's sake, "Let's quit while we're ahead."

The two girls thanked him and returned to their parents. He returned the guitar to Owen, who seemed at a rare loss for words.

Reggie gave a yawn, and Adrienne stifled one of her own. She faced a long shift beginning in a couple hours.

After excusing herself from Harper, she drew Reggie aside. "I have to take a nap," she said. "You seem tired, too."

"Am not!"

"I'll be glad to watch him," Wade said. "You go rest."

Adrienne didn't argue. With this man, she no longer felt a need to maintain tight control over her nephew or her home.

"You and the kids were really special." She couldn't leave without telling him that.

Wade's strong face warmed. "It was fun."

She barely covered her mouth in time to hide another yawn. "I'll be downstairs by seven." It was nearly six now.

"I'll put stuff away as best I can," he told her. "With Reggie's help, of course."

His son leaned against his father. "Yeah."

Sleepily, Adrienne climbed the stairs. The wedding had gone beautifully. A mellow feeling of satisfaction propelled her to her room, where she undressed, slid beneath the covers and instantly fell asleep.

A GENTLE HAND on her shoulder roused Adrienne. For a disoriented moment she thought it must be morning, and then she jolted awake. The clock showed 7:10 p.m.

"You said you had to be up by now." Wade set a cup of coffee on the bedside table. "I thought this might help."

"I must have turned off…" She'd forgotten to set the alarm, she realized. "Thank you. I hate oversleeping."

"I'm sure some zealous nurse would have called."

"She'd only be doing her job." Pulling the covers around her for modesty, Adrienne reached for the coffee. "This is just what the doctor would have ordered if she hadn't been so absentminded."

Wade chuckled. Seated on the edge of the bed, he seemed in no hurry to depart, and until she'd drained the cup, Adrienne wasn't eager to kick him out.

In keeping with the wedding's fall colors and casual atmosphere, he wore a brown jacket over a gray knit shirt and tan slacks. On the patio, he'd almost faded into the background, but his air of calm alertness reminded Adrienne that she'd once pictured him as a crouching lion.

"Nearly everyone's gone," he told her. "We packed a bunch of leftovers in the fridge."

"Those belong to the bride and groom."

"They took some," he assured her. "We folded the chairs and tables and put everything on the patio in case of rain. Not that there's any in the forecast."

"The caterer will collect them tomorrow afternoon." She'd given instructions to enter through the side gate. "Where's Reggie?"

"He and Mia are helping the groom's mother with the dishes."

Everything was in order, thanks in large part to Wade. The only downside was that the rumors already circulating must have gained a quantum boost. "Did people ask what you were doing here?"

"I told them you hired me as your butler." He kept a straight face until Adrienne nudged him with her sheet-clad knee.

Wade flashed a boyish grin. It went straight to her head, or was that the caffeine?

One more sip and she'd be finished. Adrienne wished she could roll over and close her eyes for a few minutes. *Or pull this handsome guy down on the bed and show him what I'd like to do with my butler.*

Good thing he couldn't read her mind, she mused as she downed the last swallow.

"In the morning I'd like to take Reg with me while I check out a place to rent," Wade said. "My dad and I reached a parting of ways."

"I'm sorry to hear that." Any breach in a family was unfortunate. "Was it about his drinking?"

"Basically, yes." Wade didn't object to her nosy question, Adrienne noticed, but neither did he elaborate. "Maybe I'll try one of those weekly suites near the hospital until I find something long-term."

In the cozy circle of her bedside lamp, with the empty cup warming her palms, Adrienne felt like inviting him to stay here. They had two extra bedrooms, and Reggie would be delighted. Having Wade on hand would simplify her life in countless ways.

*And complicate it beyond measure.*

In addition to her attraction, which surely she had enough willpower and good judgment to control, lay a bigger issue: her nephew's sense of stability. Who could tell whether they'd prove compatible roommates or how long Wade would stay? And suppose he found another woman to share his bed and possibly his future?

"That sounds like a plan." Adrienne set the cup aside.

"I talked to your friends about the properties they're vacating, as you suggested." Wade took the cup and rose. "The rents are a bit higher than I can pay. But at least I've started my search."

"Good." Adrienne watched his well-built body stride

from the room. As the door closed, the air quivered with his indefinable scent—part soap, part pure masculinity—tempting her to call him back.

But she'd made the right decision by letting him go. Firmly, she tossed the covers aside and went to dress for work.

THE PATIENT, A twenty-one-year-old unmarried college student named Judi Finnegan, had been in active labor for six hours, Adrienne noted on the chart. Her cervix was five centimeters dilated and 70 percent effaced, or thinned—still not ready for delivery—but she was 100 percent distraught.

"Just get it over with!" she was shouting at the nurse when Adrienne entered the room. There was no one else present—no family, no father, no labor coach.

"The contractions are four minutes apart, Doctor," the nurse told Adrienne. "She hasn't had any childbirth classes but she's refusing to consent to an epidural during delivery." The local anesthetic would relieve her pain while allowing her to stay alert and participate in the birth process.

The pain having receded, the young woman collapsed on her bed, face turned away from the monitoring equipment that showed her and the baby's heart rate. Her jaw was set stubbornly.

After introducing herself and asking a few questions—Judi merely grunted in reply—Adrienne asked the nurse for a minute alone with the patient. She pulled over the guest chair.

"If we administer an epidural, it will ease the pain," she said. "I gather you object?"

Light brown hair drenched with sweat, Judi took a couple short, shallow breaths. "If it doesn't hurt, I might not hate it."

*And I thought I'd heard everything.* "You mean the baby?"

A tight nod was the answer.

Despite her dismay, Adrienne refrained from lecturing the young woman about the miracle of life. The chart said she was estranged from her parents and that the father wasn't involved.

"Is there anyone I can call to help you through this?" Adrienne asked.

"No," Judi said angrily. "I've decided to give it up for adoption. I don't want to see it. I don't want to care about it."

"Have you made arrangements with adoptive parents?" They might provide support.

"Not yet. Can't someone else take care of that?"

The hospital had a social worker on staff. "I'm sure we can work that out."

However, the fact that Judi hadn't contacted anyone regarding adoption, combined with her present agitation, indicated she wasn't at peace with her decision. Adrienne respected mothers who chose to surrender their infant to a loving home, but if this patient gave the infant away without confronting her conflicted emotions, she might suffer lifelong trauma.

"For now, let's focus on your delivery," she told the young woman. "My medical advice is to have the epidural. It will reduce your blood pressure, which is a little high, and ease the workload on your muscles and lungs."

Tears ran down Judi's round cheeks. "My boyfriend said he loved me and we'd raise our child together, and now he's gone."

"Some men are like that," Adrienne sympathized.

"I told my parents to stop trying to control me. Now that Brian's gone, I won't beg them to take me back. They'll use it against me for the rest of my life." Judi's muscles tightened, viselike. "Not again!"

After summoning the nurse, Adrienne said, "You don't have to suffer like this when you deliver. Think about having that epidural, okay?"

There was no answer. Leaving the young woman with the nurse, Adrienne went to check on her other laboring patients.

A short while later she was pleased to learn that Judi had agreed to the local anesthetic. Adrienne returned to provide support as Judi weathered another labor pain. "You're very brave," she said after it passed.

The young woman turned her head away. "I've messed up my life. I'm such a failure."

"We all make mistakes," Adrienne pointed out.

"I had my life all planned," Judi said miserably. "Now Brian's gone and everything's ruined."

Rather than dwell on the faithless boyfriend, Adrienne noted, "Your chart says you're a college student. What are you studying?"

"Journalism." The young woman shifted to let the nurse plump her pillows.

"You can still pursue that, with or without a baby."

"I'd like to write about medical topics." Judi stopped talking to sip some water.

"Such as what you're experiencing tonight?" Adrienne said, only half joking.

The patient smiled weakly. "I used to think I'd like to be a physical therapist. Guess I'm not sure what—" Her muscles tightened once again as a fresh contraction hit. Adrienne held her hand while a nurse talked Judi through the pain.

It had just ended when Adrienne's phone beeped with a message: another patient to be checked. "I'll see you in a few minutes."

"Okay."

*I had my life all planned.* The declaration replayed

through Adrienne's mind as she went about her duties. Her plans for Reggie's future had seemed cast in concrete, too.

Another beep. The pace was picking up.

As if to compensate for the previous night's lull, this shift kept her on her feet. She was more grateful than ever not to have to deal with supervising Reggie tomorrow.

Then she recalled that he'd be spending the day tagging along while Wade rented a motel suite. A man cave, most likely. They'd have a great time.

"Dr. Cavill? We're ready for you." It was the nurse assisting Judi, who'd entered the transition phase half an hour ago.

"I'm on my way."

She found the patient fully effaced and dilated and ready to push. The birth process was exhausting but, thanks to the epidural, not agonizing.

The little girl's muscle tone, color, reflexes, heart rate and breathing all fit into the normal range on the Apgar scale, and she weighed a healthy seven pounds eight ounces. "Do you have a name picked out?" asked a pediatric nurse.

"No!" Judi answered fiercely. The nurse blinked in surprise.

Normally, Adrienne would have placed the baby on her mother's stomach while the nurse dried the newborn and covered her with a blanket and tiny cap. Instead, she asked, "Do you want to hold her?"

For a moment, she thought Judi might shout another refusal. Instead, the girl asked, "Can I wait?"

"You bet." With a nurse's help, Adrienne clamped and cut the umbilical cord and collected a tube of blood from it for testing.

How she longed to cuddle the little plum-colored cutie with her wrinkly skin and head still cone shaped from passing through the birth canal. Instead, she released the nameless baby to be taken to the nursery.

Adrienne didn't dwell on the irony that babies were so often born unwelcome. If she'd become pregnant as an unmarried girl, she wasn't sure what she'd have done, either.

At 6:00 a.m., two hours before her shifted ended, she put in a call to someone who might be able to assist. Then, after making the rounds of the patients who'd been admitted during the night, she visited Judi.

Alone in a double room, the young woman lay dozing. About to slip out, Adrienne paused when Judi said, "Dr. Cavill?"

"Hi." She stepped closer. "How're you doing?"

Large hazel eyes fixed on her. "You must think I'm awful."

"I think you're doing your best to make the right choice," Adrienne corrected.

"Maybe I deserve this." Her mouth quivered. "A few years ago I was a volunteer here. There were all these girls showing up to surrender their babies 'cause they confused the name with the Safe Haven law. I thought it was a funny story and I told my cousin at the newspaper about them. Like it was some kind of joke. Now the joke's on me."

What an exaggerated sense of guilt this poor girl carried. "Listen, there's someone I'd like you to talk to."

"Who?" Judging by the suspicious tone, Judi feared Adrienne meant her parents.

"She'll be here any minute." Peering into the hall, Adrienne was relieved to see a tall woman heading their way, blond hair pulled into a ponytail that emphasized her sharp features.

After they greeted each other, Adrienne turned to the patient. "Judi, meet Dr. Samantha Forrest. Sam's a pediatrician who does volunteer counseling with young moms."

The patient pressed her lips together as if she might reject the offer. Then she said, "Aren't you the one they call Fightin' Sam?"

"That's me." Samantha had earned the nickname by standing up for "her girls."

"I remember how much you cared about those moms who were giving up their babies. Thanks for calling her, Dr. Cavill."

"Good luck," Adrienne said, and left the two of them alone.

An hour later, near the end of the shift, Sam stopped by to say Judi had called her parents. "Mr. and Mrs. Finnegan were overjoyed. They hadn't been able to reach their daughter for months and they've been worried sick."

Adrienne thanked her for responding so quickly. The pediatrician had a husband and family of her own, as well as a busy schedule, yet she'd set everything aside to come in early.

"Are you kidding? I'm a born-and-bred do-gooder," Sam replied cheerily.

*And I'm a born-and-bred fool,* Adrienne mused. Because it had finally hit her that she was still trying to control every aspect of her life, as if that were possible.

Maybe, like Judi, she ought to take a chance and see what happened.

## Chapter Twelve

At 6:00 a.m., a pajama-clad Reggie popped into Wade's room. "Morning, Dad! Let's do something."

Rolling over, Wade scratched his stubbly chin. While rising early on a Saturday might not be on his list of favorite activities, he had plenty of energy and a clear head. "Go get dressed, sport, and I'll do the same."

"I can make coffee," the boy said brightly.

That startled Wade. "You know how?"

"I've watched Aunt Addie. I can figure it out."

Wade pictured coffee grounds everywhere and a resulting brew either thick as cheese sauce or thin as a perp's alibi. Not to mention the possibility of burned hands or a broken carafe. "Tell you what." Wade swung his legs out of bed. "Let's eat out instead."

Never mind the refrigerator full of food. They'd save that for dinner.

"Waffle Heaven, okay?"

The restaurant, a few blocks from Fact Hunter, had been a favorite in Wade's younger years. "You bet."

"Yay!" His son sped off.

Since Reg had taken a bath last night, Wade commandeered the shower in their shared bathroom. Hot water sluiced over him, banishing the last trace of sleep.

Afterward he put on jeans and a plaid shirt. If Adrienne were there and on a normal schedule, he'd brew that coffee and serve it the way he had yesterday. How silky and tousled she'd looked with her hair spread across the pillow. And when the sheet slid low, no red-blooded male could have missed the upper swell of her breasts.

Realizing his body was hardening, Wade steered his thoughts in a safer direction. After breakfast, they had a couple chores to do. The first of those might prove interesting indeed.

Downstairs, he left a note as to their plans. Despite a wish to stick around and say hello when Adrienne arrived, he figured she might appreciate some privacy.

Reg wiggled happily beneath his seat belt as the black coupe glided to the restaurant. Feeding him sweets for breakfast didn't fit Wade's idea of good nutrition, but he believed in tempering a healthy regime with mercy.

And what a treat it was to eat at the restaurant, even though they had to wait ten minutes for a table. The delicious smells and the jovial sound of dishes rattling and families chatting were better entertainment than any TV show.

He barely glanced at the menu before ordering the Walnut Maple Surprise. Reggie went straight for the Triple Chocolate Dream.

While they waited for their order, Wade explained that he'd left his father's place. "Later today I'd like you to help me take a look at Harbor Suites."

"Okay." Reggie, who'd been angling his spoon to study his own reflection, dropped it on the tablecloth. Wade half expected him to renew the invitation to stay at Adrienne's, but instead he asked, "What did you and your dad fight about?"

Kind of a heavy subject, but the kid deserved an answer. "Remember I told you Daryl is an alcoholic?"

"Uh-huh."

"He used to be a sheriff's deputy," Wade added. "That's like a police officer. He had to quit because of his drinking."

The waitress appeared, setting down a glass of milk for Reggie and refilling Wade's coffee cup. He waited until she was gone before continuing.

"The other night, my father asked me to recommend him for a job with the detective agency where I work." Wade gazed sadly into those young silvery eyes so much like the ones he saw in the mirror every day. "I had to tell him no. You have to be trustworthy and sober to be a detective."

"I bet that made him mad." Reggie heaved a sigh too big for his little body. "Do you think it would help if I talked to him?"

Wade nearly burst out laughing, but turned it into a cough. His son must have heard that phrase spoken more than once by his aunt and her friends. "I'm afraid he's too far gone for that."

After a resigned nod, Reggie sipped his milk.

Wade's gaze swept the surrounding tables. Some of the diners were couples; many were families with children. Whether laughing or scowling, chatty or silent, none of them led charmed lives, he felt certain, yet he hoped few had had to absorb this kind of adult information at such an early age. Still, in a few years, Reggie might be offered alcohol by other kids. With luck, he'd remember what he'd learned about its consequences.

Their orders arrived. Halfway through they switched plates and enjoyed their meals with renewed fervor.

"Where are we going now?" Reggie asked when they were done.

"Next stop is Phil's Garage." In his haste to pack, Wade had left some important items, including his camera, in a drawer at Daryl's. He'd emailed his father, who'd tersely promised to bring them to work this morning. It was nearly eight, the time the garage opened. "I have to pick up a few things."

"Doesn't your dad work there?"

"That's right."

Reggie's forehead puckered. "I get to meet him?"

"We'll see what mood he's in." *Or if he shows up at all.*

WITH NO PATIENTS close to delivering, Adrienne was able to leave at the scheduled end of her shift. On the way home she rehearsed what to say to Wade. First she'd take him aside out of Reggie's hearing. Next— Well, she wasn't sure.

*It occurred to me that since we have two extra bed-rooms, it's a waste of money for you to rent a place.*

That sounded as if she were taking pity on a pauper.

*You've been so helpful. I don't know why I didn't simply ask you to move in last night.*

Too pathetically grateful, as if *she* were the charity case.

*How would you feel about staying here for a while?*

Over-the-top casual, as if he were a weekend guest.

She was too tired to think properly. Still, they should have this discussion as soon as possible.

At home Adrienne immediately noticed the silence. It was a little past eight. Could they both still be in bed?

In the kitchen, Wade's black handwriting dominated her scratch pad. "Gone to eat & run errands."

Gone.

With that single word, how empty the house became. No high eager voice punctuated by a deeper one, no foot-steps on the stairs, no expectation of rounding a corner and seeing Wade's face.

Oh, heavens, she had it bad. Adrienne sank down at the table and wondered if she ought to rethink this whole idea.

BEHIND PHIL'S FRONT counter, a teenage girl glanced up from the tabloid she'd been reading. On closer inspection, Wade realized she was much too young for this job, which meant she was most likely Phil's twelve-year-old niece filling in for the regular clerk on a holiday weekend. The girl lived with her uncle and grandmother, Daryl had said.

"You must be Kelli." Wade introduced himself. After a glance outside to confirm that Reggie was still in the coupe, he asked, "Any sign of my father?"

"Nope. You could call him."

"I'd rather not."

"You guys aren't speaking, huh?" she asked with interest, flicking back long brown hair laced with pink-and-blue strands.

"We email," Wade told her. "That's close enough." His father refused to text, contending his big fingers always hit the wrong letters.

"Well, he's not here, but he left this stuff for you." She produced a small bag from behind the counter.

Inside Wade found the camera and other items he'd requested. "Thanks."

"No problem."

Through an open door to the garage bays, he saw Phil working on a pickup truck. Sure enough, no Daryl. "Did you see him when he came by? I wondered what condition he was in."

"The bag was here this morning when Uncle Phil and I arrived," Kelli explained.

"My father has a key?" That showed a remarkable amount of trust.

She shook her head. "He left it outside the door with your name on it."

"That camera cost… Never mind." Wade scowled.

"You want some advice?" the girl asked.

A twelve-year-old offering to counsel him? Now, that was funny. All the same, Wade assumed a somber expression. "I'll take what I can get."

"My dad died in Iraq," she said. "Spend time with your father while you've got him."

Those were wise words, regardless of her age. "Good advice."

"Oh, who's the little cutie?"

Wade turned to see Reggie peering inside. "Hi, guy." No sense scolding him, especially since this conversation had taken longer than expected.

The boy scuffed his shoe. "Is Grandpa here?"

"Not today." After introductions, Wade steered his son out of the office. "Dad left my stuff, so we're done here."

"Oh, okay."

Hearing Reggie's disappointment made Wade even angrier at his father. But the kid was lucky. If Daryl had been there, hungover, there was no telling what unpleasant things he might have said.

In the car, Wade took out his cell. "Let me call the Harbor Suites and find out if the manager can show us one of the units."

BUSY SIGNAL. ADRIENNE scowled at the phone. And Reggie wasn't answering his, which probably meant he'd put it on vibrate and couldn't feel it over the movements of the car. He set it that way at school and often neglected to change it.

If she didn't reach Wade soon, he was likely to rent a suite for the next week or two. While that didn't preclude his joining them later, an inner urgency pushed her to settle the matter now.

Despite her reservations, Adrienne had concluded that inviting him to live there made sense. These were the holidays, a period when she missed her family more than ever and when the lack of grandparents was especially painful for Reggie. Having his father around would be comforting as well as convenient.

Once she got this conversation over with, she'd stop worrying about it. To pass the time while waiting to redial, Adrienne jotted notes about how to organize meals and schedules.

She had no idea how long the arrangement would last or how they'd adjust if—no, when—Wade began dating. She'd simply have to be flexible.

She tried his number again. It still went to voice mail.

ALTHOUGH NO ONE answered Wade's repeated calls, he stopped by the motel anyway and spotted the manager on a ladder, stringing Christmas lights across the one-story front unit. The grizzled fellow finished hooking the end of the strand before descending to greet Wade and Reggie.

"I usually forward calls to my cell," explained the man, who gave his name as Mr. Lopez. "The darn thing rings pretty loud, though, and I don't care to risk tumbling off a ladder."

"I can show you how to put it on vibrate," Reggie piped up.

"Can you, squirt?" Mr. Lopez's grin revealed a silver tooth. "I never feel the vibrations, though."

"Me, neither," the boy admitted.

"We'd appreciate your showing us a suite," Wade put in, to move things along.

"When were you planning to…? I wonder who that is." The man squinted at a blue sedan stopping at the curb. "Always perks up my day to see a pretty lady."

"It's my aunt!" Reggie cried. Sure enough, that was Adrienne at the wheel. The little boy trotted over.

"Hi, sweetie," she said to her nephew. As she approached, hand in hand with Reggie, her skin glowed in the mild winter sunlight. The brightness in her expression touched Wade; he could hardly believe she'd worked all night. "I hope I'm not intruding."

"Mr. Lopez was about to show us a suite." Puzzled, Wade awaited an explanation for her unexpected appearance. She tilted her head toward the manager, indicating she'd rather not speak in front of him.

Mr. Lopez, apparently not noticing her gesture, motioned them toward the courtyard. "Right this way."

After a brief hesitation, Adrienne followed him. Wade set aside his curiosity. Since this didn't appear to be an emergency, he'd find out soon enough why she was there.

THE SUITE HAD a plainly furnished front room, a kitchenette and a bedroom that Adrienne didn't bother to examine. There was nothing terribly wrong with it. And nothing very right, either.

Close to her, Reggie whispered, "Where will I sleep?"

"We'll discuss that later," she answered.

Wade's face betrayed little, but by now she knew him well enough to note his lack of enthusiasm. "A few holiday decorations might spruce it up."

"Oh, this unit is spoken for." The manager regarded them apologetically. "I was about to tell you—the folks are arriving this afternoon. We don't have a suite available till next week. We do have single rooms, though."

*Here's your cue.* "That settles it," Adrienne announced. "You should stay with Reg and me."

Wade gave a start. "Seriously?"

"Why not? We have two empty bedrooms." Did that sound ungracious? Still, in front of the manager, she chose to keep this impersonal. In a way, she was grateful that his lack of a vacancy had provided an opening for her suggestion.

Hopping with eagerness, Reggie chimed in, "Say yes, Dad!"

Wade didn't answer right away. Surely he wasn't keen to stay at this depressing motel; he wouldn't have been even had a suite been available.

"I suppose it will be hard to find an apartment during

the holidays," he said slowly. "Sure, that would be great. Sorry we wasted your time, Mr. Lopez."

"It wasn't wasted." He kept an appreciative gaze on Adrienne. "I'm always happy to show such nice people around."

In the parking lot, after tucking Reggie into the coupe, Wade accompanied Adrienne to her car a few spaces away. "What's this about?"

She didn't blame him for wondering. "Having you move in with us… Well, I decided to go with the flow. Your phone was busy and I was afraid you might put down a deposit."

She couldn't read much in the emotions flickering across his face. Finally, he said, "It'll be fun for Reg, for the holidays. I won't take advantage of your hospitality any longer than necessary."

"It's okay." Her chest felt tight. Although he'd accepted, his guardedness wasn't encouraging.

Wade tapped her door lightly, as if marking an end to the conversation, and strode back to his son. She'd done the right thing, Adrienne was convinced. She'd also been correct to assume he didn't want a relationship beyond the collegial one they'd established.

*Stop trying to control the future.*

Together they'd create a memorable holiday for Reggie. And then, whether she liked it or not, Wade would be on his way.

## Chapter Thirteen

Wade had never lived in a big house like Adrienne's. And he didn't exactly live there now, even though he'd moved his stuff into the spare bedroom. As a temporary resident, he still felt like a hotel guest—a nonpaying one.

Perhaps that explained why, during the two weeks since arriving, he'd done his best to maintain a low-key presence, putting away every dish and smoothing the couch after watching TV. Aside from leaving a few personal articles in the bathroom he shared with Reggie, he confined his possessions to his own room.

Also, while they'd agreed on ground rules about noise, meals and schedules, he kept stumbling across things he hadn't considered. Adrienne forgot to warn him that she employed a cleaning service twice a month, and Wade narrowly escaped major embarrassment that morning when he darted from the bathroom to retrieve the clothes he'd left in the bedroom. Wrapped in a towel, he nearly mowed down a lady wielding a dust cloth.

"Sorry," he said, whipping into his room. He'd believed he was alone in the house.

She merely stood there openmouthed. After he came out, he introduced himself, and they both pretended not to notice each other's red faces. Thank goodness he'd thrown on the towel by instinct.

Someday he'd like to have a home like this. Even better,

he'd like to share it with his son. Yet Adrienne's willingness to let him move in, even temporarily, showed a huge amount of acceptance on her part.

He was grateful to have this chance to get to know them both better. Being a father involved a major learning curve, and the role, he was beginning to understand, would evolve as his son grew.

At the office, Wade's change of address drew a few raised eyebrows. Sue Carrera went around all day grinning, no doubt anticipating another staff romance.

She couldn't have been further off base. Adrienne was polite, friendly, but distant. Her moments of sadness reminded Wade that her sister had died nearly a year ago. He had his own painful memories connected with this season, but he hoped that as Christmas drew closer, they'd both rally for Reggie's sake.

For the upcoming weekend, she suggested bringing down the artificial tree from the attic. That, he hoped, would mark the start of festivities and a renewal of the closeness he'd experienced during the wedding. Wade could hardly wait.

That Friday he was called into Mike Aaron's office. Wade remained standing in front of the broad desk until his boss finished reading something on his laptop. Glancing up, Mike removed his glasses and closed the computer. "Have a seat."

Since he'd been expecting a performance review after a month on the job, Wade sat rather stiffly in one of the chairs. While he'd completed each project and had his reports approved with only minor corrections, he took nothing for granted.

"I have a rather unusual assignment for you." Mike scratched his thick thatch of hair.

"Unusual?" This might be a test, Wade considered.

"The client requested you specifically." His boss leaned

back, stretching his long legs under the desk. "Not only that, but he refuses to discuss the details with anyone else."

Who might put in such a request? "Did he explain how he knows me?"

"That wasn't necessary." Mike seemed in no hurry to provide more information. He had a gift for turning small issues into power trips.

"I see." But of course, Wade didn't.

"The client is Bruce Hunter."

*What?* Wade swallowed, aware that his astonishment showed despite his attempt to match his boss's self-control. "My grandfather is hiring me? He didn't even want me to work here."

"Apparently he's changed his mind." Having obtained maximum shock value, Mike moved on. "He'd like you to stop by his condo so he can fill you in. Anything he tells you is strictly confidential."

"He does realize that you'll be reading the report, right?" Wade asked.

"Yes, but he specified that we're not to mention it to anyone else at the agency."

This must concern Daryl. But if Grandpa had questions, why not just ask Wade straight-out? Or did Bruce suspect Dad of being up to something suspicious? If he was, Wade had seen no sign of it while staying with his father.

He accepted the slim folder Mike handed him, which contained Bruce's address and background information. As if he needed it. "I'll start right away."

Mike waited until he was halfway to the door before asking, "Aren't you interested in your performance review?"

Wade turned sheepishly. "I was wondering."

His boss didn't drag things out. "Flying colors. You'll see a slight raise in your next paycheck. I wish it were larger, but we're still getting this business off the ground."

"Much appreciated."

"Glad to have you here."

In the report-writing room, Wade called his grandfather. Bruce answered on the second ring.

Wade identified himself, repressing the urge to add, "Reporting for duty, sir." This was a real case, and despite the positive feedback from Mike, one positive performance review didn't make him immune to criticism. "Is this a good time for me to stop by?"

"No," said the gruff, familiar voice. "Tomorrow."

That was inconvenient for Wade, since he'd planned to spend the morning with Reggie and had promised to help Adrienne with holiday decorations after lunch. If he refused, though, he could imagine Bruce's belittling response. Real detectives worked on weekends or whenever else they had to.

He took the initiative. "Three o'clock would work for my schedule."

Loud throat clearing preceded Bruce's reply. "I guess if you're tied up till then, that will do." A harrumph was followed by, "What do you hear from your father?"

"Not much." Since their argument Wade and Daryl had exchanged only a few brief messages on practical matters. "Why are you asking me? I thought you two were on good terms."

"I can't stand listening to his slurred speech when we talk and his lies about taking cough medicine," Grandpa said.

"He and I don't get along so well, either," Wade admitted.

"We're just one big happy family, aren't we?"

That didn't bear commenting on. "I'll see you tomorrow at three." Unsure how to address his grandfather in this situation, Wade avoided using any name.

"Done." With that terse conclusion, Bruce hung up.

As he pocketed his phone, Wade realized what the conversation signified. His grandfather wasn't hiring him to snoop on Daryl. If so, why had Bruce asked about him on the phone?

Whatever the old guy was up to, Wade would have to wait to find out.

ON SATURDAY MORNING as she was leaving the hospital, Adrienne noted a text message from an unfamiliar account. The subject line read "THX From Judi."

That was the young woman whose daughter she'd delivered two weeks ago, to whom she'd given her cell number. "My parents will help me raise her," Judi wrote. "Her name's Merrie, for Xmas. She's so sweet. Look!" Attached was an image of a darling baby in a pink onesie, cuddled against her mother's cheek.

Adrienne's eyes burned with tears as she replied. She felt happy for Judi, glad for the chance to help and a deep yearning for what could never be.

*Stay in the moment.* This month she'd had to fight her impulses since Wade had moved in. It was hard not to touch him, not to join in playful tussling with him and Reggie, not to show how much she yearned for him.

But she'd managed. And she would keep right on managing, Adrienne resolved, and headed for her reserved parking spot.

Already the new routine felt familiar. She arrived home to find the laundry running and enjoyed a leisurely breakfast without having to worry about Reggie's supervision for the day. After touching base with Wade, she went to bed and slept soundly.

As usual, she awoke at lunchtime. Although that didn't give her a full night's sleep, she'd napped for several hours in the on-call room, and she had a couple days off to catch up.

The door cracked open and Reggie peered in. "You awake?" he whispered.

"I am," Adrienne confirmed.

Into the hallway he hollered, "Okay, Dad! We can bring down the tree now!"

A light tap preceded Wade's appearance behind his son. "Should we wait till you're up?"

"Go ahead and get started." The physical chore of carting stuff from the attic held no appeal for Adrienne. "I'll join you shortly. The pull-down door to the attic is in the ceiling next to your bathroom."

"I noticed." He gave her an indulgent grin.

"Set up the tree in the family room," she added.

"The front hall has more space."

"But it isn't as friendly." Adrienne didn't mention her other reason for placing the tree in a less-public spot. Over the years, it had lost some of its artificial needles and much of its freshness. She'd planned to dispose of it after the holidays last year and buy a new one, but Vicki's death had thrown everything off-kilter.

"Point taken." In front of him Reggie was hopping from one foot to the other. "Okay, sport, let's give your aunt some privacy."

"Can I climb up the ladder?" Reggie asked, darting under his father's arm.

"Yes, but carefully, and only when I'm watching." Wade gave Adrienne a wink before closing the door quietly.

Once Adrienne showered, dressed and ate a quick meal, she found that the industrious pair had already set the tree on its stand in a corner of the den. Boxes of ornaments, wreaths and knickknacks lay on the coffee table and carpet.

Nostalgia rushed over her. Years ago she and Vicki used to tumble about while their parents decorated a tree—a real one. The scent of pine had filled the air, along with apple cider heating on the stove and cookies baking.

Only a little over a week remained before Christmas. Recovering from the wedding and adjusting to her new housemate, she'd fallen behind in her planning. She'd meant to update the collection of ornaments, and she hadn't yet wrapped presents.

Wade was checking the colored lights intended for the porch. "Most of these are burned out. I'll buy a new string, but not today. I have an appointment with a client in a little over an hour."

"You're working?" She felt unaccountably disappointed.

"I'm afraid so." He shrugged. "Not sure how late this will run."

"Hope you make it home for dinner," Adrienne said. "I'm cooking pasta with broccoli and peanut butter."

"My favorite!" Reggie put in. Adrienne was sure half a dozen other dishes would have drawn the same response.

"Save some for me, okay?" Wade gave her a sideways smile. "I'll be hungry whenever I get home."

"Of course."

They spoke like roommates or friends, yet a sweet tension hung in the air. *We're always tiptoeing around each other.* Was it possible he had feelings for her, too?

If so, Adrienne reminded herself, they couldn't afford to indulge them. For Reggie's sake, the two of them had to work together. To be strong, dependable and stable. There was no room for the emotional roller-coaster ride she had experienced during her long-ago engagement and that Wade had apparently suffered with Vicki. Presumably any other love affairs hadn't worked out, either, since he'd remained single.

They both had terrible track records. Mercifully, they'd begun to form a workable team. That was enough.

Since the exterior lights weren't ready to hang, they devoted their energies to the tree. Adrienne's favorite ornaments were the personal ones: framed pictures of Reggie as a baby and toddler, salt-dough figures he'd whipped up in preschool and kindergarten, and a coffee-filter angel

Vicki had helped him create last year. There were a scattering of colored glass balls, tiny toy soldiers and wooden elves, as well.

She explained the history of each to Reggie. While listening, Wade settled a large old-fashioned Santa on the top. He was tall enough to reach it without a ladder.

Next Wade affixed sparkly angels to the higher branches. "Is anything here from your own childhood?"

Adrienne hesitated to comment in front of Reggie, but it was better to give him the facts. "My father drank too much one year and knocked over the Christmas tree. Stuff broke."

"That was bad," Reggie said. "People shouldn't drink."

"You're right." Although some doctors recommended a glass of wine with dinner, Adrienne considered it wise for a person with a family history of alcoholism to avoid even that.

As usual, Reggie's attention quickly shifted. "Can I take photos now?"

Startled, Adrienne regarded the bedraggled tree. It was hardly worthy of recording, yet this was a special holiday for her nephew. After a tough year, he had his father. And she'd like to build up a new stock of family photos, even though they couldn't entirely replace those they'd lost. "Sure."

The little boy ran for his camera. Harper, who took professional-quality photos of insects and hummingbirds to illustrate children's nature books that Peter wrote, had taught Mia and Reggie to compose their pictures, study the lighting and use special settings.

The boy was absorbed in his picture taking when Wade departed. "I'll replace the lights as soon as I can," he promised.

"Thanks." *For being here. For bringing us light in more ways than one.* "Good luck with your client."

"I may need it," he said enigmatically.

"We'll be baking cookies this afternoon." The fragrance would fill the house. "I'll save you a plate."

"What kind of cookies?"

"Does it matter?"

"Studies have found chocolate chip to be vastly superior to any other cookie on earth," Wade informed her. "Aside from that, I'm not particular."

"I'll keep it in mind." She nearly walked him to the door, except that he wasn't a guest.

Then Adrienne turned to Reggie. Sticking to her theme of staying in the moment, she put all those rampant male vibrations out of her head. "Let's start baking cookies," she suggested.

Lowering his camera, he faced her solemnly. "What kind?" he asked, just like his father.

"All kinds," Adrienne said, grateful for her stock of refrigerated dough.

"Yay!" And with that unqualified endorsement, off they went to the kitchen.

THIS TIME, SOMEONE had locked the gate at Bruce's condo complex. Wade buzzed his grandfather, who promptly let him onto the grounds.

Good start. Expecting to encounter hostility, Wade wouldn't have been surprised had Bruce kept him standing there like a fool.

As he strode between buildings, the wreaths and lights already glimmering in the late afternoon reminded him of what he was missing at Adrienne's house. In Pine Tree, Wade had volunteered for holiday shifts and served at charity kitchens to avoid the loneliness of his silent apartment. This year, sharing the small ritual of decorating the tree had soothed his spirit.

No decorations enlivened Bruce's door. However, scarcely had the bell rung before it opened.

Bruce stood erect, his crisp cotton shirt and slacks tailored to his thin frame. Giving Wade a taut nod, the elderly man stepped aside to admit him.

Wade kept his expression blank as he entered the living room. He'd have shaken hands, but his grandfather didn't offer one.

*He hired you to do a job, nothing more. Don't treat this as personal.*

Bruce eyed him sternly. "I presume you realize this business is between you and me and no one else."

"Except my employer." Wade remained standing since he hadn't been invited to sit.

Grandpa acknowledged the comment with a tilt of the head. He coughed and then continued, "Here's the thing. I'm not the sort of man to put up with a woman who cheats, you understand?"

Startled, Wade registered that the case concerned the mysterious girlfriend. "I do."

"I'd drop her in a minute if I figured she was like that, but it seems out of character." Bruce scowled. "She claims to love me, but she turns off her phone and doesn't return my calls for hours. Won't tell me where she's been. You see the problem."

*The problem is that you're in love with her, or you'd already have said sayonara.* Wade took out his pad and pen. "What's her name?"

"Renée Green."

That sounded familiar. Hoping the connection would surface, Wade went on asking questions and jotting information. Address. Age, height, approximate weight and where she worked.

She was retired and volunteered at the hospital. Since hospitals restricted the use of cell phones, that might explain why she wasn't always available by phone, although not why she kept her whereabouts secret.

They'd met about six months earlier at a summer con-cert at City Hall Park, where Bruce had offered Renée his folding chair, Wade learned. The next weekend, they'd at-tended an Angels baseball game, and since then they'd spent several evenings a week together.

However, Bruce hadn't met her friends, and she hadn't met his. Each paid separately for meals and tickets, except when she cooked a special dinner or Bruce treated her to a movie. If the woman had secrets, Bruce hadn't been able to find any clues on the internet. He'd also checked her credit rating, which was sterling. A widow, she owned her home.

She didn't strike Wade as a gold digger. Nor did she can-cel dates, make hysterical middle-of-the-night phone calls or otherwise act unstable.

The photo his grandfather provided revealed a woman in her mid-sixties with strong features, a rectangular face and graying brown hair. Nothing overtly flirtatious marked her appearance, and kindness shone from her eyes.

"Does she have children?" Wade inquired.

Bruce hesitated before answering. "One married son. And a grandson."

"Her son's name and address?" An even longer pause followed. As Wade waited, he remembered where he'd heard her name before. No wonder his grandfather had gone to such lengths to keep the matter secret from the other detectives. "It's Lock Vaughn, isn't it?" Mike's part-ner had said his birth mother volunteered at the hospital.

"Yeah. Don't raise a fuss about it," Bruce grumbled.

Although he'd done no such thing, Wade refrained from correcting the client. This was understandably a sensitive subject.

"Let's discuss indications that she might be cheating," Wade said. "Has her behavior toward you changed re-cently?"

"She's grumpier than usual," Bruce muttered.

"Less affectionate?"

"Not once she's warmed up."

That might be more information than Wade cared to know. However, he was there in a professional capacity. "Does she accuse you of cheating?" That was a common tactic used by unfaithful partners.

"Wade, I was a detective before you were born," Bruce snapped. "I know all this crap."

*Hang on to your temper.* "How often is she unavailable?"

"More than she ought to be."

This seemed to mark the end of the interview. "I'd appreciate your giving me an idea of her usual activities and schedule," Wade said. "I'll start surveilling her right away."

"Tonight," his grandfather said. It wasn't a question.

"That would be fine."

While his grandfather wrote down the requested information, Wade ran a background check on Renée using a web service to which the agency subscribed. Aside from filling in a few details, it added little to what he'd already gathered.

Saturday evening did seem like a prime time for the amorously inclined to entertain company, Wade acknowledged as he departed. After calling Adrienne to tell her not to save his meal and grabbing some food at a drive-through, he located the target's house in a residential area a few blocks from the medical center. With its gingerbread trim and multipaned windows, the cottage resembled a fairy-tale illustration. A lit nativity scene on the lawn showed restraint compared to the overblown displays of Santas, reindeer and cartoon characters on neighbors' lawns.

Wade parked across the street and a few doors down. Scrunching in his seat, he kept an eye on the place while staying alert for dog walkers and other potentially snoopy folks.

As twilight fell, lights came on inside the cottage, revealing a cheerful room lined by china cabinets. Occasionally, he caught a glimpse of a woman moving about inside. As far as he could tell, she was alone.

After a couple hours, Wade's limbs had stiffened and his back hurt. Stretching, he was about to call Adrienne just to talk when a faded sedan halted in front of the house.

Might be a neighbor. Or not.

A man emerged from the driver's side. Middle-aged, perhaps ten years younger than Renée, he wore a thin jacket and seemed nervous. The guy stood on the street, studying the house—too bad Wade couldn't see his face from this angle—before approaching. Admiring the decor? Preparing to greet his lover? Planning a heist?

Wade readied his camera.

A flash of light from the doorway revealed the sturdy frame and unmistakable face of Renée Green. Wade started snapping pictures, on alert for an embrace.

Bending down inside the doorway, the woman lifted something from the floor and handed it to the man. It was a grocery bag, a canned ham visible above the rim.

The passenger-side car door slammed and a tiny girl pelted up to the porch. Wade photographed Renée bending for a hug. Then, toting a sack labeled The Bear and Doll Boutique, she accompanied her visitors to their car.

Wade ducked lower.

Through his partly open window, he heard the rumble of the man's voice and caught a few words of Renée's response. "I'm glad your wife's recovering."

She must have met these people at the hospital and decided to brighten their holiday. Wade wondered what his surly grandfather had done to deserve such a saint. But generosity didn't preclude the possibility that Renée had a dark side he just hadn't stumbled across yet.

The visitors drove off. Once his target returned indoors,

Wade headed out. It was cold and he preferred not to remain in one place too long.

Despite what he'd witnessed, he was far from concluding that Renée had nothing to hide. She was dodging Bruce while continuing to claim she cared about him. If Wade couldn't find an explanation for her behavior, he'd be failing his grandfather.

Worse, Wade would be letting down his boss. And that he did not intend to do.

## Chapter Fourteen

"You bought him a sweater?" Stacy sat up on the examining table, her amber eyes dancing with mischief. "A sweater, for the man you're living with? I never took you for a romantic, Adrienne, but seriously!"

*We shouldn't be discussing personal matters during office visits.* That wasn't Adrienne's real problem, though. It was that despite her insistence that she and Wade remained nothing more than housemates, her friend refused to believe it. So did half the hospital staff, according to the gossip she'd overheard.

"What's wrong with a sweater?" inquired Cole, who'd accompanied his wife to her checkup. Since Adrienne saw private patients from 6:00 to 8:00 p.m. three nights a week, he hadn't had to rearrange his own schedule.

"There's nothing wrong with a sweater." Hearing the sharp note in her voice, Adrienne switched topics. "Stacy, you're doing very well. It's impressive that you've carried the triplets to within six weeks of your due date. They're growing well, your blood work came back normal and your weight gain is within the desirable range."

"Really? I feel like the side of a barn." Stacy had been suitably distracted, thank goodness. "My sister claims she never gained more than twenty pounds with any of her four children."

"Who were singletons," Adrienne pointed out. "Are you

staying off your feet as much as possible?" She didn't press for complete bed rest, once a common recommendation in multiple pregnancies, because it hadn't been proved to prevent preterm labor.

"Yes," Stacy said.

"No," her husband responded.

"I am, too!"

"We closed escrow on our house last week," Cole told Adrienne. "She's been packing."

"While sitting down!"

"Scheduling the cleaning crew, the movers...."

"On the phone," his wife insisted.

"Try to cut back," Adrienne advised her patient. "Also, be sure to wear compression stockings and elevate those swollen ankles."

"Okay, okay. They'll go down as soon as I deliver anyway."

"A little knowledge is a dangerous thing," Adrienne replied. "Just because you're a nurse doesn't mean you're immune to complications."

"That's what I keep telling her, but she won't listen," Cole complained. "When she was my surgical nurse, she used to treat my observations with more respect." He appeared more puzzled than offended.

"You've been demoted from Lord High Surgeon to husband. But that's also a promotion," Adrienne explained.

He looked mystified. "Is there a point at which all this will make sense to me?"

"Unlikely."

She and Cole were assisting Stacy to her feet when her friend reverted to her earlier theme. "I'm still amazed that Wade turned out to be the opposite of what Vicki used to tell us. He's such a doting dad! At the wedding, when Una let him touch her bulge and the babies moved, he practically levitated."

"She let him touch her abdomen?" Cole asked. "Where was her husband?"

"Sitting right there, in a fog."

"I'd never allow that," he muttered.

"You'd never notice," she teased.

Usually, Adrienne enjoyed her friends' exchanges. Tonight she was glad when they left. The reminder that Wade would want more children kept her keenly aware of the knife's-edge balance in their relationship.

The sweater she'd bought him was thick and soft, a shade of blue-gray that would complement his eyes. Before wrapping it, she'd stroked the texture and imagined it fitting over his broad shoulders. Absorbing his scent. Becoming part of him.

Then she'd folded it into a box and said goodbye to it. Well, not entirely. Since she had Christmas Eve and the next night off work, she'd be there to open presents no matter what time they chose. But after that... Well, she had to stop thinking of Wade as belonging to her.

She'd hardly seen him the past week since he'd been busy at work. While he'd managed to buy replacement holiday lights, he hadn't yet strung them on the porch. He'd promised to do that by tomorrow night—Saturday—and suggested the three of them handle the task together.

"I'll need someone to steady the ladder," he'd told her with a teasing smile.

"Of course," she'd said. "Reggie's too small to do that."

"Right." He'd seemed almost disappointed, as if he'd expected her to flirt a little. "That reminds me, I'd better go wrap my presents before he decides to explore my closet. Have a nice evening."

"You, too."

Now Adrienne shook off the memory. She had more patients to see before her overnight shift.

*Presents to wrap...* Had he bought her anything? And if so...

If so, it must be something practical. Just like what she'd bought for him.

DESCENDING THE LADDER, Wade checked to be sure Reg was standing at a safe distance. In his concern not to accidentally bump his son, he missed a step and hit the ground hard.

Instead of ducking aside to protect herself, Adrienne grabbed him. "Are you all right?"

"Hurt my ankle a little." Embarrassed by his mistake, Wade hesitated to let her support him. But when he leaned on her, it felt good.

"We should go ice that joint," she said.

He'd rather stand there, relishing her softness and the freshly shampooed fragrance of her hair. "I'll be fine."

"I can put the ice on it," offered Reggie.

"You know how to do that?"

The little boy's face scrunched in concentration. "Kind of," he said. "Can we use ice cream?"

"Afraid not, sport. Besides, why waste it?"

"I'll apply the ice," Adrienne said. "And then I have a selection of Ace bandages."

Wade refused to act like an invalid. "Here's a better idea. Now that we've contributed to the major energy drain on the western United States, let's drive around and look at other people's lights."

"We used to do that when I was a kid," Adrienne said wistfully. "It isn't dark enough yet, though. And if you're in pain, don't try to be a hero."

"I'm fine." Wade preferred to move on to the fun stuff. "Where did you stop to eat when you were a kid?"

"The Cake Castle!" cried Reggie.

Both adults stared at him. "That's a bakery, not a res-taurant," his aunt remarked.

"Mommy used to take me there for lunch."

Wade winced. *Only when she was out of control, I'll bet.*

"There's Krazy Kids Pizza." Adrienne's tone lacked enthusiasm.

"Can we, Daddy?" Reg asked.

Wade had a better idea—and a good excuse. "They're carryout and delivery only," he said. "But while we're on the subject of Italian food, let's hit Papa Giovanni's."

No one argued. The restaurant was famous for its hearty and delicious Italian cuisine, ranging from pizza to gour-met specialties.

Although it was scarcely half past four, they were hun-gry, and with no other tables occupied, they got fast service. Wade supposed that from keeping such odd schedules, he and Adrienne were both accustomed to snatching meals when they could.

After downing pasta and salad, they piled back into the sports car. Wade drove toward the harbor, which had seemed magical to him as a child. From Harbor View Road, they caught a breathtaking glimpse of lights spar-kling around the curve of water, from houses on both sides as well as from yachts and smaller boats at anchor. On the inland bluffs, lights flashed and twinkled on the mansions.

"It's so elegant," Adrienne breathed.

"Beautiful," Wade agreed.

"Like stars fell to the ground," Reggie piped in from the backseat.

Poetic, Wade mused. And true. "Now for a change of pace."

"What do you mean?" Adrienne asked.

"You'll see."

In Renée's cozy neighborhood, people didn't try to im-press anyone with their subtlety. Many crammed their lawns, roofs and porches with gaudy animated figures and riotous blinking messages of goodwill.

Wade knew the best spots because he'd put in many hours around there. So far, he'd found no sign of a secret lover and no explanation for Renée's continuing to keep her distance from Bruce except when on a date…or, in one instance, spending the night. He hoped he'd discover the explanation soon, because Bruce was running out of his limited stock of patience.

Within a few minutes, they were cruising between bright lights. Wade glided to a stop in front of one house with a blinding display and a sign instructing them to tune the radio to a special channel.

"Here goes." Wade followed the instructions.

Another car stopped nearby. Then a van slotted into place in front of them.

"What's going on?" Adrienne studied the sign. "These people put on a light-and-sound show?"

"Cool!" Reggie cried happily. "Like the videos."

"Which videos have you been watching?" Since the little boy wasn't allowed to surf the web, Adrienne sounded understandably wary.

"We watched them together," Wade explained. "They're strictly G-rated."

"Oh. That's fine, then."

"Here we go," he said, and turned up the volume.

Over the radio boomed a rock version of a Christmas carol. The lights began flashing in time, transitioning between minilights on the bushes, a tree covered in white, a panel of lights on the roof and lit plastic sculptures of reindeer and Santa on the lawn. The pulsing beat was so irresistible that soon the three of them were bouncing hard enough to rock the car.

Adrienne laughed, her joy contagious. Reggie squealed

with glee. As for Wade, he wished he could capture this moment to savor forever.

When it ended, Reggie shouted, "More!"

"Too much of a good thing quickly wears thin." Wade suspected the experience would lose its magic if repeated too soon.

"Let's go home," Adrienne concurred. "This was fun, though."

Home? The evening didn't feel over. Suddenly Wade realized why. "Let's buy a Christmas tree."

"We have one," Adrienne pointed out.

"Let's buy a real one," he said. "The kind that smells wonderful, sheds needles and has to be carted out to the curb afterward." To address another potential argument, he added, "We can leave the old one in the den and put the new one in the hall."

"Two Christmas trees?" she murmured.

"There's no law against it."

"Please, Aunt Addie?" Reggie pleaded. "That would be so cool."

Wade held his breath, waiting. This meant more to him than he'd expected.

A smile broke through Adrienne's reserve. "Let's do it."

While a cheer went up from the backseat, Wade put the car into gear. He'd seen a tree lot in the northern part of town, near the freeway, and there they went.

This close to the holiday, the selection proved thin but adequate. They chose a small well-shaped tree, along with a stand and a box of multicolored glass balls.

The pine scent infusing the lot carried Wade back to childhood Christmases, until an old pain hit him like a blow. He recoiled and strained to put it out of his mind. He'd rather replace old memories with new.

After all, this was his first holiday with his son, who skipped happily between the trees, scooping up handfuls of pine needles and tossing them. Then Adrienne slipped her hand into his as they walked to the counter to pay for their purchases.

It was like having a family again.

At home they stabilized the tree in the hall and hung the ornaments. Reggie began yawning, and despite his grumbling, they ushered him off to bed. Wade had barely begun reading a favorite book when Reg fell asleep.

"He's exhausted," his aunt observed as they went out.

"He'll be bouncing off the walls tomorrow all over again." Wade had learned that much about his little guy.

In the hallway, Adrienne said in a low voice, "Thank you. This was a special evening."

"For me, too."

She indicated his leg. "How's the ankle?"

"Better." Except for a few twinges while tromping around the tree lot, it hadn't troubled him.

"It might stiffen overnight," she warned. "Let's put an Ace bandage on it just in case."

"Sure thing, Doc." Wade hoped she'd do the honors.

Adrienne disappeared into the hall bathroom but reappeared empty-handed. "I guess they're in the master bath."

"I'm not used to having someone take care of me," Wade admitted as he followed her.

Reaching the entrance to her bedroom, she regarded him teasingly. "I can't understand why not. You're kind of cute."

"Cute?" He arched an eyebrow.

"Well, you must have been a cute kid once," she amended, and ducked inside. Since she left the door open, Wade took that as an invitation.

Her personality colored the generous-size room, from the orange-red poppies on the curtains to the matching quilt on the queen bed. Adrienne's light fragrance filled Wade with a sense of belonging and intimacy. He yearned for more.

In her bathroom, Adrienne rummaged through a drawer before producing an assortment of compression bandages, each tucked into its original box. "Here's one for the wrist... elbow...aha! Ankle."

"Why so many?" Wade asked.

"My mother and sister had a tendency to trip and fall," she said ruefully. "Of course, Reggie takes the occasional tumble, too. And I get my share of strains. Delivering babies is a physical business."

"Police work is, too," Wade noted. "But I tend to push through the pain."

"Macho."

"And proud of it."

"Well, unless you plan to balance on one foot while I do this, Mr. Machismo, you'd better take a load off."

On her vanity table, an array of bottles sparkled like jewels. In front of them, Wade perched on a chair covered with delicate golden fabric and, half-afraid the fragile thing might break beneath his weight, leaned down to unlace his shoe. "This is great."

Kneeling with the wrap, Adrienne regarded him curiously. "What is?"

"The way the light... This whole..." His heart squeezing, Wade stopped. The memories he'd tried to banish flooded in, sharp and dangerous. "Damn."

"Your ankle's throbbing?"

"Not that." He'd guarded his darkness for so long he could barely imagine revealing it. But if he didn't, he'd have to maintain a wall around himself and keep her at a distance. He wanted to move beyond that point. "Being here reminds me of before my mother left. Before all the brightness went out of my life."

Adrienne rocked back onto the carpeted floor. "Will you tell me about it?"

"I don't want to burden you."

"Believe me, you won't." She rested her hand on his knee.

It chafed at Wade to show anyone his scars or, in this case, the wounds that had never completely healed. Yet he had to share them with Adrienne so she'd understand him. "When I was thirteen, she left Dad and me for another man. Her note said..." His voice broke. Fiercely, Wade forged on. "She said she'd only stayed because her son needed her, and now..." His eyes burned. "Now, instead, she was getting in my way."

Adrienne's touch on his leg anchored him. "In your way? How?"

Wade swallowed. "I'd been going through a stupid adolescent rebellion. Treating her like the enemy. Staying out late with my friends, complaining about her cooking, acting like a jerk."

"You blame yourself?" she asked gently.

*Yes.* "It was like she rejected us both, and the worst part is I deserved it." The story didn't end there. "I was angry about being abandoned. She married again and traveled a lot with her new husband, visiting his son and grandkids and seeing the world. I only met them a couple times."

"But you stayed in contact?"

"Aside from a few brief visits, we only occasionally talked on the phone, but it made Dad furious. He considered her a traitor, and since he was the only parent I had left, I sided with him," Wade admitted. "By the time I figured out that I shouldn't be expected to choose, it was too late."

As if recalling that she had a task to do, Adrienne began wrapping the stretchy bandage around his ankle. "What do you mean, too late?"

"When I was sixteen, she and her husband were flying in his private plane to spend the holidays with his son in Lake Tahoe," Wade said. "A storm came up and the plane went down in the mountains. There were no survivors."

Her hands stopped moving. "How sad. You never had a chance to say goodbye."

"Later, when I was training for police work, I talked about it to a counselor," Wade said. "That eased some of my feelings, and I buried the rest. But they still resurface, especially this time of year. If only I'd tried harder to reach out or hadn't been such a jerk to her in the first place."

"You believe she'd have stayed?" Adrienne secured the bandage around his ankle. "That she'd have ditched her lover for your dad?"

"I suppose not. But maybe she'd never have taken up with him in the first place." As he spoke, Wade saw how childish his thinking was, assuming that he could have saved his parents' marriage if he'd only been good enough.

"Last year when Vicki went out drinking on New Year's Eve and smashed her car into a tree, I blamed myself." Adrienne returned the empty bandage box to the drawer. "Although she was sober when she left here, I knew she'd soon start drinking. I tried to take the keys, but she grabbed them away. I wish I'd done more. Tied her up, called the police…."

"There's nothing they could have done while she was sober," Wade said. "And you had no legal right to restrain her."

"That's what I try to tell myself."

"How about Reggie? This was obviously hard on him, and still is." He'd seen that in his son's behavior the day they'd visited the cemetery.

"I took him to a therapist afterward," she said. "I went, too. But while grief counseling can help, it doesn't entirely banish the pain."

"How about the guilt?" Wade asked. "Because for me, that's almost as bad."

"Reggie doesn't seem to suffer from that. But I do. I guess that growing up in families like ours, we feel like we should be able to fix everything." The glitter in Adrienne's eyes matched his own tear-blurred vision.

"How do you deal with that?"

"I try to remember that we can't make choices for other people. And we'll never be perfect. We can only do our best, take each day as it comes and forgive ourselves for honest mistakes."

Inside, a hard knot dissolved. Hearing the words in Adrienne's soft voice gave them power.

The power to heal. And the power to bring the two of them together.

Impulsively, Wade reached for her hands and rose, drawing her up. "I need you," he said, gathering her against him. With her hair flowing around him and her mouth inches from his, they were lost in a private, precious world.

"I need you, too," she whispered.

After that, there was no more room for words.

## Chapter Fifteen

Wade's hard body fit against Adrienne's as if he'd been designed for her. She loved the roughness of his skin, the restrained strength in his muscles and the tender way he gazed into her eyes before kissing her.

Although both had experienced other lovers, she sensed they'd been alone so long that every touch had become new. Peeling off each other's clothing, adjourning to the bedroom, exploring each other as they rolled and teased and cuddled, was almost like the first time.

When his intensity grew, she met him with a passion of her own, taking what she wanted. He clearly liked it when she played the aggressor, then turned the tables and flipped her on the bed. They were partners, sharing their reactions, their excitement rising even as they strove to delay the moment of union as long as possible.

*Never let this end.*

Adrienne's only hesitation came when Wade murmured something about protection. While she was trying to frame a response, he scooted out of bed and retrieved a condom from his wallet.

"It's kind of old." He regarded her apologetically.

"That's okay." Putting every other consideration out of her head, Adrienne unrolled it over him with the exquisite skill of a surgeon.

Eyelids half-closed, Wade moaned. She caressed him, thrilled to be arousing him. Then it was his turn to trace fire across her body with his mouth.

They merged like two people coming home. It was right and natural, and inevitable. Then rioting sensations blotted her awareness of anything but Wade—his eagerness, his caring and his explosive climax.

Glorious waves rolled through Adrienne. Never before had she been lifted to such heights. Wade's fierce thrusts melted the last of her resistance, and she soared. With him, beyond him.

*Never end. Never end. Never end.*

But when it did, her body eased into shining mellowness. Blissfully, Adrienne nestled against Wade's shoulder as he pulled the covers over them.

HE'D NEVER BEEN in love, although he'd mistaken infatuation for love once, fleetingly. Waking in the early-morning light, Wade recognized how little he'd understood.

When you loved someone, you cared as much for her happiness as for your own. You shared a private world, and you almost didn't mind that you'd have to be parted occasionally, because you'd always come home to her again. You didn't have to erect walls to protect your heart, because she was on the inside with you.

One thing aroused his curiosity. When he'd mentioned protection, Adrienne had stiffened. Was she keen on having children right away? He wouldn't mind, except that pregnancy could be hard on a woman. But to bring another child into the world, well, how fantastic.

The clock read 5:22 a.m. Too bad his body didn't automatically adjust to a Sunday schedule, Wade mused. Unwilling to get up, he leaned over the side of the bed and took his cell phone from his pocket. He'd been meaning to order an instructional guitar DVD for Reg. Might as well do that now.

Soon he was quietly surfing the web.

ADRIENNE AWOKE IN the gray morning light. There should be sunshine to match her mood, winter or not. Stretching contentedly, she peered up at Wade, who sat absorbed in a tiny illuminated screen.

Typical male, she thought indulgently. "Morning," she said.

"Back at ya," he teased.

A quick check assured her that they'd closed and locked the door last night. Any minute Reg might come bounding down the hall.

Sitting up, Adrienne glanced at Wade's phone. Abruptly, the air in the room chilled. Why was he studying a website about baby clothes and nursery furnishings?

"What…" Her throat closed, and she had to swallow before continuing. "What's that about?" *Please tell me you're buying a present for Cole and Stacy.*

Warmth suffused his face. "I have to admit, you've opened a new world to me. I never thought past having my son, but now…"

"You want a baby." She struggled to keep her tone even.

"Only if…" He left the sentence unfinished. "Hey, no hurry. I don't mean to rush things, but I've changed these past few months." Setting the phone aside, he shifted toward her. "With you, with Reg, I've learned a lot about myself and that I really love being a father. Thinking about what you do at work, what your friends are experiencing, that would mean the world to me." He reached out and stroked her abdomen.

He couldn't have hurt her more if he'd slapped her. *Tell him now,* Adrienne thought.

The pain ran too deep. She'd finally opened up to a man,

grown to love and trust him, only to learn that she'd made a terrible blunder. And it wasn't even his fault.

*I should have been honest sooner.* But she'd never meant to let their relationship develop this far.

She moved away. "Wade, I'm sorry."

"For what?" He studied her uncertainly.

"Last night…" She hurried on, afraid to stop because she might lose her nerve. "It was a mistake."

His eyes narrowed. "What are you talking about?"

"Not entirely a mistake." Adrienne hoped she sounded more coherent to him than to herself. "We're compatible physically. That's obvious. The thing is, we share so much, from our backgrounds to our devotion to Reggie, that…we shouldn't confuse that with love. With building a future."

Anger flared on his face, as if he'd been stabbed in the back. Which, she supposed, he had been. "You can't mean that."

"I do." *Liar, liar.*

"Why are you saying this?" He shook his head. "Granted, I don't know much about women, but I'd have sworn—"

"Please accept my decision."

"What decision?" he demanded. "You're tearing us apart for no reason just when we're coming together. Sharing a house, sharing a bed."

Feeling her back to the wall, she instinctively fought harder. "Did you miss the part about our living arrangement being temporary?"

"You're throwing me out?" Wade asked in disbelief. "Adrienne, we need to talk about this."

"I can't." Her throat constricted. She hadn't intended to make him leave, but every instinct commanded that she protect herself. The longer she waited, the greater the devastation.

"Have you thought how this will affect Reggie?" he demanded. "Let's give it a chance."

"I have a right to say no." She swallowed. "You should respect that."

"But…"

In the hallway, she heard Reggie's footsteps. "We can't let him find us like this. It will make everything worse."

His jaw tight, Wade swung out of bed and grabbed his clothes. He disappeared into the bathroom.

The doorknob rattled and held. "Aunt Addie? Why'd you lock the door?"

Adrienne's chest hurt. It took all her self-control to rise, pull on a robe from a chair and hurry to the door.

She gazed down at her nephew's sweet little face, bright with morning enthusiasm. "Guess I pressed the lock by accident."

He accepted the excuse without question. "I'm hungry."

"Let's fix breakfast." Swinging the door shut behind her, she steered her nephew toward the stairs.

WADE REPLAYED THE conversation in his mind as he showered in the hall bathroom, where he'd scooted as soon as he heard their voices safely downstairs. He still didn't understand what had happened. Adrienne's rejection was beyond comprehension. He'd trusted her. Loved her. And assumed she felt the same.

He must have projected his emotions onto her. Misread her completely. Now he mistrusted all his reactions where she was concerned.

One thing was clear, Wade decided as he switched off the water. As much as he hated being separated from his son, Adrienne had a right to make him leave her house. He'd have to work extra hard so Reg wouldn't feel abandoned.

If that was possible.

WHEN WADE ENTERED the kitchen, Adrienne had no idea what to expect. Anger, most likely, yet he appeared cool, guarded and in control. Also utterly desirable, a sweatshirt defining his chest and jeans hugging his lean hips.

If only he would meet her gaze, but he didn't.

"Hi, Dad!" Reggie waved a spoon, sending milk droplets across the table. Adrienne mopped them with her napkin. Normally she'd have pointed out his carelessness, but she didn't trust herself to speak.

"Hey, sport." At the counter, Wade filled a bowl with cereal. "Listen, remember that suite we looked at?"

"Sweet?" Reg repeated.

"Like an apartment." At the table, his father poured milk into the bowl, avoiding Adrienne's gaze.

"Uh-huh." The little boy sounded puzzled.

"Well, they called and they have a unit ready for me." Wade's smile lasted barely a millisecond. "I have to move in today or they'll give it to somebody else."

The motel hadn't called, Adrienne thought miserably. Wade had phoned them. But she had no doubt the rest was true. And it was her fault.

"It's the holidays!" Reg protested.

"Here's how I calculate it," Wade continued. "I'll be moving there today. Tomorrow night—that's Monday—you can sleep over with me and give Aunt Addie a break. Tuesday's Christmas Eve, and she has the night off, so you guys can celebrate together. The next afternoon, I'll pick you up after lunch and we'll open presents at my new place."

Under the table, Adrienne clenched her fists. She hated this, his leaving. Yet she'd brought it on herself.

"I want to spend Christmas with my family," Reg argued. "My *whole* family. Dad, don't go."

Anguish etched lines into Wade's face. She was hurting him and hurting Reggie, Adrienne saw. But blurting out the truth was hardly a solution. At this point it might make things worse.

At least he'd offered a workable plan. And he hadn't

used his ultimate threat. He could still most likely prevail in court and take her little boy from her.

She trusted him to rise above that. But the possibility terrified her.

"Reg, my staying here was always meant to be temporary," Wade told him. "Just until I found a place where you could stay overnight. The timing's lousy, but we'll all adjust. I'll be right here in town, and we'll see each other on Saturdays and…other days."

"No!" Tears ran down Reggie's cheeks. When Adrienne reached for him, he shrugged her off. "I want both my parents!"

"And you'll have us." Wade's chest rose and fell heavily. "Just not together."

"You're ruining Christmas." His face crumpling, the little boy ran past his father. Adrienne heard him thump up to his room.

Shaken, she turned to Wade. "I'm sorry that he's blaming you."

He lifted the spoon to shovel cereal into his mouth and then set it down still full. "I'm honoring your request."

"Maybe…" She wasn't sure how to finish that sentence.

Wade looked straight at her, finally. "Let's not fight. Let's not unload on each other the way my parents used to do. I'm not sure about yours."

Adrienne nodded. Her parents had staged their share of wrenching battles.

"Let's get through the holidays as best as we can and keep things friendly for Reggie's sake," he went on. "It's lucky my father and grandfather weren't expecting any festivities."

"Once Reg gets used to the idea of you living nearby, he'll be fine." She hoped that was true.

"He needs us both," came his taut response.

"Then we'll make sure he has us both."

Without further conversation, Wade dumped his cereal in the trash and went out.

How could she have gone so quickly from utter happiness to heartbreak? Adrienne wondered. And how had she managed to wreck the holidays for everyone?

She'd figure something out, she told herself as she rose to clear the table. Somehow, she always did.

## Chapter Sixteen

If Renée Green was trying to drive Wade crazy, she couldn't have done a better job of arranging her activities the afternoon and evening before Christmas.

He'd have preferred to postpone further surveillance for a few days, but Bruce refused to hear of it. After receiving Wade's preliminary report finding nothing suspicious, the old man had wielded his sarcastic tongue with a vengeance. Wade's detective skills must be severely lacking, he'd snarled, since Renée's behavior had become increasingly erratic and contradictory.

According to Bruce, sometimes she accepted his calls or returned them promptly, and other times he heard nothing for hours. She'd sweetly promised to cook a big brunch tomorrow but refused to spend Christmas Eve with him, giving no reason.

If this were simply a personal matter for Wade, he'd have told his grandfather to stop pestering the woman. Either she was planning a surprise—unlikely, given that Bruce hated surprises and Renée hadn't shown any interest in party stores, fancy restaurants or other entertainment venues—or she was ill suited to be dating such a rigid guy.

However, Wade had a job to do. And he was trying his best.

He logged nearly an hour outside the Sexy Over Sixty Gym directly downstairs from his own agency. He parked behind a large RV and was grateful he didn't get spotted by any colleagues.

Then he put in two hours outside the Oahu Lane Shelter, which was holding a pet-adoption event. Wearing a blue volunteer's uniform, Renée occasionally appeared in the front to greet arrivals and hand out flyers. While Wade admired her kindness and was glad to see animals finding new homes, did two dogs have to mark his tires as they passed?

Renée's next stop proved even trickier: Lock's house on the east side of town. Spending the evening with her son, grandson and daughter-in-law meant she was probably not up to anything questionable. Nevertheless, stung by his grandfather's insults, Wade resolved to keep an eye on the place. After all, she might spend half an hour here and then head elsewhere.

Just his bad luck—the only free parking space on the block was directly in front. And if Lock glimpsed Wade, there'd be awkward explanations that might breach confidentiality. Already stiff from his afternoon's work and growing hungry after finishing the last of the snacks he'd brought, Wade sank down in his seat.

*Well, what else did you have to do tonight?*

Two days ago he'd moved into his new digs and done his best to spruce up the place, literally, with a small pine tree. Even though he'd strung lights and baubles and placed a couple wrapped presents underneath, the display reminded him of some feeble office attempt at holiday decor.

During their Monday-night sleepover, Reggie's attempts to act cheerful failed to reassure Wade, because whenever the boy believed himself unobserved, he drooped like a wilting poinsettia. They attended a new animated film, chuckling occasionally while the families around them roared with laughter.

Camping out in Wade's living room in sleeping bags was

fun, but Reg retreated into moodiness on the early-morning drive home. *Home.* When Wade delivered his son to Adrienne's cream-and-blue house, its broad porch and array of flowers struck him as paradise lost.

He carted his son's possessions to the front and then moved to the sidewalk until the door opened. Her blond hair and flowing robe haloed by the light, Adrienne reminded him of a dream. Standing there, she gazed at him longingly. Or maybe that was pity he saw in her eyes.

He still didn't understand how he'd misjudged her so completely. Or, if he hadn't, what he'd done wrong.

Refusing to torment himself or her, he'd spun around and returned to the car.

They needed to clear the air. Perhaps tomorrow, Christmas Day, when he picked up Reggie after lunch as they'd arranged. Or, better, at a time when the little boy wasn't present.

For Reg's sake, they had to continue as co-parents. But this pain inside Wade, this ache in his heart, wasn't going to vanish overnight. While it went against the grain to open himself up to more hurt, for Reggie's sake—and his own— he meant to give her another chance to explain.

A sharp rap on the side window snapped him into the present. *Caught napping. Damn.*

The face glaring at him through the glass belonged to Renée Green. With a sigh, Wade rolled down the window.

"I don't know who the hell you are," Renée snapped. "But I know *what* you are. You're a private detective and Bruce hired you, right?"

No use arguing. "That's right."

"You'd better show some ID or I'm calling the police."

Why wasn't she calling her son, whom Wade had glimpsed earlier inside the house? Keeping her private life to herself, he supposed. "Yes, ma'am." He dug in his pocket for his license and handed it to her. "It's not safe standing in the street, Mrs. Green."

She glanced around. "There's no traffic, and I don't want my son to see me. I'd rather he didn't know what a controlling jerk I've been dating."

That seemed a fair assessment of Bruce, Wade thought. "Then may I ask why you're dating him?"

Startled, she scowled at him. "I don't see that that's any of your business." Angling the license in the dim light, she studied the name. "Wade Hunter. You're his grandson?"

"Guilty as charged," he said.

"You work for my son."

He nodded.

Her eyes narrowed. "Does Lock know about this?"

"No." Wade wrestled with how much to disclose and decided the matter had been taken out of his hands. "My grandfather specified that only Mike and I were to be informed."

"Bruce hired his old agency." She released a "huh" noise. "That, I didn't expect."

Wade wished she'd move out of the street. Drunk drivers were especially a threat on holidays, even in quiet residential neighborhoods. Also, she'd begun shivering. "Mrs. Green, why don't you get in the car so we can talk?"

"And so you can roll up your window and stay warm," she retorted.

"That, too," he responded mildly.

With only a brief hesitation, she stomped around the front of the car. Wade cleared his papers and camera off the passenger seat and stuck them in back.

She folded her sturdy frame into the right front side of the sports coupe. The scent of apple cider and cinnamon drifted from her. "Cramped, isn't it?" she grumbled.

"Sorry about that." Now, how could they deal with this business? "I'd appreciate if you'd clue me in as to why you're dodging Bruce. I have to fill out a report and my client isn't going to be pleased if I come back empty-handed."

"He's your grandfather. He'll forgive you."

Hoping he didn't look as uncomfortable as he felt stuffed in here with this angry woman, Wade said, "That doesn't mean he cuts me any slack."

"I should have figured that." A streetlight played over the silver glints in her brown hair. "Bruce has plenty of redeeming qualities. He can be amusing and tender. But I refuse to account to him for every moment of my day."

"Why not tell him that?"

"I've tried. He says he understands, and then he keeps calling." She clenched her hands in her lap. "I figured when I refused to cooperate, he'd get the message."

"You aren't trying to break up with him?" Wade asked.

"No, but I might have to."

Frustration fired through Wade. "You should be talking to him instead of giving him the runaround. How do you think it'll look in my report? Girlfriend communicates by refusing to communicate."

"Don't make me out to be the bad guy!"

"I'll just present the facts, ma'am," he said with a trace of irony. "But if it's any consolation, Bruce must be fairly smitten to go to all this trouble."

"All the trouble of harassing me?" She took his irony and doubled it.

*She's as stubborn as Bruce. What a couple.* "If you care about someone, don't play games. Instead, establish boundaries. When you see him again, tell him that if he doesn't respect your privacy, you'll be gone permanently. Set specific limits on how often he can call. Make him earn his way back into your life."

Renée's mouth tightened as if she were about to argue. Then she clicked her tongue. "Well, well. Who'd have figured Bruce's grandson had so much insight?"

"I assure you, I don't…" His phone vibrated in its dashboard holder. He'd secured the device because California banned using a handheld phone while driving. With an impatient breath, Wade glanced at the readout.

Why was Adrienne calling on Christmas Eve? Puzzled, he excused himself from Renée, pressed the phone icon and spoke over his wireless connection.

"What's up?" In the background over the phone, he heard the clattering and buzzing typical of a hospital. But she was supposed to have the night off.

"Reggie's missing." She was breathing hard, close to hyperventilating.

"What do you mean, missing?" Wade had been picturing the pair cozily ensconced at home. "Where are you?"

"Stacy went into labor with the triplets and the doctor on duty couldn't handle it all," Adrienne answered shakily. "I left Reggie with Harper and Peter for a few hours. He seemed fine."

In the passenger seat, Renée's expression grew concerned. Well, Wade couldn't keep his private life out of this. Nothing mattered now except his son's safety.

The story tumbled out of Adrienne. "Reg was playing with Mia and went to the bathroom. When no one was watching, he sneaked out of the house. Harper and Peter tried to reach me, but I was in surgery."

Wade's brain raced. "Have you tried calling him? Or if his phone's on vibrate, the police can locate his cell. Did you notify them?"

"Harper did." That was good, he registered. "They found Reg's phone near the bus stop. He must have dropped it."

The bus driver had noticed a little boy climbing on board alone, she explained. When Reg calmly announced that he was going to visit his father, the driver hadn't found that suspicious.

*Why didn't he call me to pick him up?* But Reg must have

figured Wade would only tell him to stay with Harper until Adrienne came home. *And I probably would have.* "Did he reach my motel?" There was a bus stop on the corner.

"He must have been confused. He got off several blocks too soon, according to the driver, and the police can't find any sign of him," Adrienne said tearfully. "Peter went to your complex and talked to the manager, and he's staying there to watch for him. Harper and Mia are at my house in case he goes there, but…I just got out of surgery. I called you as soon as I heard."

"They should have told me right away."

"Harper didn't have your number."

He squelched the impulse to blame. Adrienne hadn't done anything wrong. Well, rejecting Wade, maybe, but his hurt feelings were immaterial. "I'll cruise the area around the motel. Exactly where did he get off?"

After filling him in, Adrienne was about to hang up when Wade recalled the reason she'd gone to work. "How's Stacy?"

"Came through with flying colors," she said, a little more calmly.

"And the triplets?"

"Two boys and a girl. Healthy weights, and their vitals checked out fine. They're under observation in neonatal intermediate care, but they should be able to go home in a few weeks."

"I'm glad. Call me if you hear anything." He also took down phone numbers for Harper and Peter.

"Of course."

Wade struggled to think clearly. While there'd been no indication of foul play, the image of his son wandering around lost in the darkness terrified him.

"What's wrong?" Renée demanded.

Wade had almost forgotten about her. "I'll take care of it," he said tightly. "I need you to leave now."

"Don't be an idiot," she said. "I want to help. So will Lock and your bullheaded grandfather."

She was right. The more people searching, the better their chances of finding his son quickly.

Wade sketched the situation and sent her a picture of Reggie from his phone. "I'm on it," Renée said, and left.

As he put the car into gear, Wade reflected that he liked this new lady in Bruce's life. Then he steered a course across town, his adrenaline pumping.

TALKING TO WADE, knowing that he'd be searching for Reggie, eased Adrienne's fear, but only marginally. Why hadn't she paid closer attention to her little boy and his determination to be with his dad?

She'd give anything, do anything, to keep him from harm. If he really wanted to be with Wade, then that was the way it had to be. *Just let us find him safe.*

Embarrassed, she discovered that tears were pouring down her cheeks. Paige, who'd kept a discreet distance in the doctors' lounge, hurried over with a box of tissues. "I called Mike," the redhead informed her. "He plans to pack our baby in the car and drive around the harbor and along the beach just in case Reggie wound up there."

"Thanks." Adrienne blew her nose. "I should go."

"Don't drive until you're in better shape," Paige advised.

"I can't just sit around."

Paige's phone rang. "Dr. Brennan," she answered, and listened for a moment. "How far along is she?"

It must be the charge nurse, Adrienne thought. Someone else had come in. Did they have enough physicians to handle everyone?

"Yes, keep Dr. Rayburn here and call in… Who's next on the list? Dr. Franco?" That was Paige's partner, Nora, who must be at home with her husband and preschooler. "Una's her patient. She'll come." Paige ended the call.

Una Barker, pregnant with twins, was only a few weeks ahead of due date. Still, if the hospital really needed more hands, Adrienne had to pull herself together. "I'll stay."

Paige frowned. "As soon as we make sure Nora's available, you're leaving, if I have to arrange for Mike to drive you home himself."

Not Mike... Wade. The two of them ought to join forces. They'd be more effective that way, Adrienne thought. No matter how angry he was at her, surely he'd work with her today.

"I have a better idea," she told her friend, and took out her phone.

## Chapter Seventeen

While he drove, Wade called the police watch commander, who remembered him from his stint there. No, they hadn't found Reggie or anyone who recalled seeing him after he got off the bus. They'd put out a BOLO bulletin—Be On the Lookout—and officers were cruising the school and other spots that might be familiar to him. They'd also requested a bloodhound from another agency but hadn't secured one yet.

Calls to Peter and Adrienne turned up nothing new. Wade dismissed their apologies. This wasn't their fault.

Two months ago Wade's son had been little more than a photograph and a vague idea of a boy. Since then he'd become a unique and unforgettable individual. Wade didn't love him just because of their connection or because of his paternal instincts. He also loved his son for his own sake, as an incredible person who would grow up to be a wonderful man.

He had to admire Reggie for seizing the initiative. All along, the boy had shown an eagerness to jump into adult responsibilities, along with a tendency to overestimate his readiness. Unfortunately, that attitude had backfired on them all today.

Waiting for a red light, Wade got another call from Adrienne. Hoping for good news, he answered quickly. "Any word?"

"No, but would you mind picking me up at the hospital?" she asked. "I'd like to help search. I mean, if it's not out of your way."

"Of course not." The only other person in the world who loved Reggie as much as he did would understand Wade's feelings, anchor him and possibly spark ideas about where to search. Besides, he'd prefer not to have Adrienne behind the wheel when she was upset. While Wade might be distressed, too, he had experience driving under difficult circumstances. "Where should I meet you?"

"I'll be out front."

"See you in ten minutes." The hospital was only a couple miles away, but he was driving slowly, scanning sidewalks and passing cars. *Just in case.*

He'd barely clicked off when the phone rang again. To his surprise, he saw his father's name on the readout. "Dad?"

"The old man called me," Daryl said. "Families have to stick together at times like this."

It was on the tip of Wade's tongue to remind his father of his refusal even to meet Reggie. But that would accomplish nothing. "You're offering to search?"

"When you were nine or ten, you took it into your head to vamoose." His father spoke clearly, without slurring. "I found you."

"Where?"

"The shooting range I'd shown you. We gave you a toy gun for your birthday and you were determined to try it out."

Wade dredged up the incident from among his long-buried memories. Mainly, he recalled his disappointment when the range manager had refused to let him into the building. "Reggie was heading for the Harbor Suites, where I'm staying, but he got off the bus too soon."

"I presume you're already searching that area. Where else might he have gone?"

Wade cited a few spots, adding, "I gave that information to the police."

"Yeah, well, I might have a few brain cells smarter than theirs," Daryl said.

There was a painful question Wade had to ask, despite his father's apparent alertness. "Are you sure you're sober enough to drive?" He braced for an angry response.

There was a beat of silence. Then he heard, "Yes, son, I am."

"Dad…"

"You're wondering if I'm lying." His father stated that as a fact rather than an argument. "I don't blame you. I'd think the same thing."

"Maybe you should stay home." That was hard to say but necessary.

"I downed a couple beers earlier today, but by now my blood alcohol level should be well below the legal minimum," was the response. "I had some major repairs to do and needed a clear head. Quite honestly, I was about to start the serious drinking when I heard about your boy. I know I don't deserve it, but I'm asking you to trust me, because my grandson's too important for me to put him in any more danger."

Wade couldn't rush over there and physically prevent his father from driving. And Daryl had always taken care to avoid racking up drunk-driving arrests. "In that case, I'm grateful for your help."

The area around the six-story medical center lay subdued in the growing darkness, Wade noted when he reached it. Few other cars were moving, and in the absence of headlamps, the white lights on bushes and buildings glimmered brightly. As for the curving patient wings, many of the windows were dark. Only the most urgent cases would be in the hospital on Christmas Eve.

In front of the lobby doors, a familiar figure paced, her

hair pulled back and her hands shoved into the pockets of her heavy jacket. Adrienne's face lit up with relief when she saw him.

As she slid into the car, Wade reached for her. Without hesitation her arms encircled him, and they clung to each other like shipwreck victims on a lonely raft.

She belonged with him, Wade thought. Maybe after tonight, she'd see that.

DESPITE HER KNOT of anxiety, Adrienne's spirits rose as she held on to Wade. She found refuge in his powerful grip, the late-day roughness of his cheek and his heartfelt welcome.

"You okay?" he murmured.

"Better now." Reluctantly sitting back, she said, "It's lucky I came out through the lobby. They were about to close the desk and lock the front doors. Just imagine if Reg showed up and there was no one here."

"He might be there already," Wade pointed out.

She'd thought of that. "Security searched the place, and I asked them to do it again." She'd emphasized the places her nephew was most likely to go, including the day-care center, where he'd stayed occasionally.

"Good." He frowned. "If the front door's locked, how do patients get in?"

"There's a separate entrance for labor and delivery patients. Visitors can use it, too, on a night like this." Adrienne fastened her seat belt as the car edged forward. "The moms-to-be tour the hospital in advance, so they're informed."

"What if Reg does show up?" Wade asked.

"The woman at the desk called one of our most dedicated volunteers, and she's coming in." A shadow moved to her right, and Adrienne gave a start. It was only a cat.

His gaze continuing to sweep their surroundings, Wade said, "Her name wouldn't be Renée Green, would it?"

"That's right." He must know Renée from working with

Lock, Adrienne thought. "She's a treasure. And she's bringing her boyfriend. Apparently he has some sort of police background and he'll search the grounds."

"It's my grandfather."

"What?" Wade had mentioned being on the outs with the man and that he'd founded the detective agency, but nothing about Renée. "How did you know…? I mean, when…?"

"Long story. Let's save it for another day." Wade stared ahead. "I want to check Harbor Suites again. Then if Peter will hang in there, we'll drive the neighborhood in a grid pattern."

"Good idea." Thank heaven he knew what to do. *And I know what I have to do.* Steeling herself, Adrienne said, "Wade, he really wants to be with you. I'm sorry if I've stood in your way."

"You're not in anyone's way." He shot her a startled glance. "Reggie wants his family. Both of us. Not just me."

Tears smarted in her eyes again. *His family. Both of us.* Wade was including her, but she still hadn't told him the truth.

In the passing glow of streetlamps, his profile had a chiseled strength. Adrienne drew courage from that as they entered the motel parking lot.

Dɪᴅ Aᴅʀɪᴇɴɴᴇ sᴇʀɪᴏᴜsʟʏ believe that Reggie would prefer living alone with him? Wade knew better. But her willingness to sacrifice what she loved most in order to make her nephew happy touched him deeply.

Why did she refuse to see them as a family? Every glance, every touch confirmed his belief that she cared about him as much as he cared about her. Well, maybe not quite. But if she'd give him a chance…

*Or are you conning yourself with wishful thinking?* That was, he'd learned, not unusual among people who grew up in alcoholic households.

At the motel, they encountered Peter pacing the walkway outside Wade's unit. Ushering him in from the cold, Wade assured him that Reggie's decamping wasn't his fault. "My son has a mind of his own."

"We should have watched more closely." Peter turned to Adrienne. "I heard Stacy went into labor. Is she okay?"

She told him about the successful birth. "Cole's floating a couple inches off the floor."

"That's fantastic." The teacher, whose muscular build testified to his extracurricular position as a wrestling coach, gave them a wry smile. "Remember my sister Betty from Maryland?"

"She's due in January," Adrienne said. How typical of an obstetrician to focus on that fact.

"She delivered a healthy little girl tonight." Peter shook his head. "I associate babies with New Year's Eve, not Christmas, but we're thrilled."

"Congratulations." Wade couldn't spare any further energy on small talk. "If you'll stand watch here, we'll cruise the area. Let's stay off our phones unless there's news, in case Reggie reaches a phone and tries to contact us."

"Understood."

Although Wade's voice mail showed no messages, he wished he hadn't had to make so many calls earlier. And he chose not to mention that every passing hour increased the risk. They were all worried enough as it was.

"Thanks, Peter." In the flat lighting of an overhead fixture, dark circles underscored Adrienne's eyes.

Wade guided her outside, steadying her with a hand at her waist. They had to find Reggie. *And we will.*

As they reached the car, he mentally plotted a route. Having patrolled this area years ago, he pictured the cul-de-sac and twisty streets into which a little boy might stray.

Tonight as he drove, the town seemed slightly distorted, like a warped photograph. What a bizarre contrast between their fears for Reggie and the cheery illuminated lawn decorations. Wade forced himself to screen out the distracting flashes and focus on any dark shape that might be a child.

Adrienne stared out her window with equal intensity. After a few blocks, she said, "Wade, there's something I need to tell you."

Although tempted to point out that this was hardly the moment for a heart-to-heart, he checked that impulse. Talking might relieve her tension. And if there was a reason for her behavior toward him, he'd like to hear it.

"What is it?" Wade kept his tone neutral.

"I know how important it is to you to have more kids of your own," she began.

What did that have to do with anything? *Don't argue.* "Go on." He tapped the brake at a stop sign and then rolled forward.

"I can't have children."

The terse statement hovered in the air. That was what had been troubling her? Wade wasn't sure how to react. "Why not?"

She drew in a long breath. "When I was young and stupid, I let my boyfriend drive me home one night even though he'd been drinking. It wasn't far. Just far enough for him to smash into a tree."

As Wade studied the shadows of the houses, he sensed other shadows joining them in the car. Dark anguished shadows from Adrienne's past. "You were badly hurt?"

"He only had a few bruises. But I… The seat belt cut into me." The words choked out. "I had to have an emergency hysterectomy."

"That must have been devastating." Wade glanced at her tear-streaked face, uncertain how to offer comfort.

The enormity of what she'd suffered hit him hard. This woman who spent her days and nights bringing other women's babies into the world could never have one of her own.

That must make Reggie all the more precious to her. Yet she'd offered to give him up.

Still, he couldn't respond without fully grasping what this meant. To her, to him, to them both. Clearly the loss had influenced her view of herself and of men all these years.

The blocks slipped by with no sign of Reggie. "How did you come to terms with that?"

"I focused on my medical studies and my career." Adrienne used a tissue from her purse before continuing. "I told myself it was lucky I wasn't torn between my work and my family like so many women doctors."

"Still, in all these years, you must have met men who could handle that, men who were worth your time." She was beautiful, intelligent and caring. Those weren't qualities Wade often encountered in an available woman.

She plunged ahead. "During my residency, I got engaged to an attending physician who claimed he'd never been interested in kids. In retrospect, I guess that wasn't an ideal situation, since I hadn't ruled out adopting, but I felt safe with him. Like we were building a future."

"I take it that didn't happen."

"He cheated on me with a nurse." A trace of anger edged her words. "She got pregnant and suddenly he couldn't wait to marry her. He went around bragging about becoming a father."

"The…" Bypassing a swear word, he settled on, "Jerk."

"In retrospect, he'd have made a lousy husband."

"Betrayal hurts, even when you're better off without the idiot," Wade said.

"Yes, it does."

They turned another corner, into another street filled with holiday decorations and Christmas trees visible through front windows. Wade slowed alongside a woman walking a dog. Rolling down his window, he called, "Have you seen a little boy about six years old?"

She regarded them with concern. "No, but I'll look for him."

"Tell the police if you spot him. They're searching, too."

"I will. I hope he turns up safe."

"His name's Reggie. And thanks." He raised the window.

Beside him Adrienne had fallen silent. She'd shared her most painful secret, and Wade ached to reassure her. But when he did, his response had to be genuine and complete. Before then he needed to deal with this knife-sharp disappointment, selfish but undeniable, that there'd never be a miraculous baby that was part him and part her. That he'd never feel their infant moving inside her.

His phone rang. The name on the readout was Daryl.

"It's my father checking in," Wade growled, and pressed the talk button. "Go ahead."

But the voice in his ear didn't belong to Daryl. "Hi, Dad!"

It was Reggie.

## Chapter Eighteen

*He's safe. He's safe. He's safe.* Joy engulfed Adrienne as she listened to Wade on the phone with his son. "Are you okay?…Where were you?…I'll let you talk to your aunt."

He switched the phone to regular mode and handed it to her. "Reggie?" She was half sobbing and half laughing. "We've been so scared!"

"I'm sorry." Her little boy sounded more excited than contrite, though. "Grandpa Daryl found me. I got lost and ended up at his garage."

"His garage?" Adrienne couldn't picture what he meant.

"Where he works."

"Oh, that kind of garage." She'd forgotten Daryl was a mechanic.

"It was closed, so I sat in front of the door where there was some warm air," Reggie said. "I'm hungry. We're going to my great-grandpa's house."

"Okay. I mean, why?" But he'd already clicked off.

Wade had stopped by the curb. Now he slid the phone into its holder and brushed a stray wisp of hair from Adrienne's forehead. "Better?"

As she nodded, tears welled up. "I don't know how I could have dealt with losing him."

"Then why'd you offer to let him live with me?" Wade's voice was gentle.

"I'd do anything to keep him safe." She plucked another tissue from her purse. "That's not the same as losing him."

He put the car in gear. "For some reason, Reggie wants to go to my grandfather's condo. I gather he's not giving up this opportunity to meet the rest of the family."

"I guess not." Through her relief, Adrienne still felt a twist of anxiety. Wade hadn't responded to what she'd told him. Yet they had other priorities. "I'd better make sure everyone has been notified."

"Good plan."

Daryl had met up with a police officer, who'd verified that the boy was safe and called off the search, she learned. Peter and Harper, ecstatic at the news, said they'd be returning home and wished her and Wade a merry Christmas. At the hospital, Renée had spread the news to the doctors and nurses. She added that Una's twins, a boy and a girl, had arrived in great shape.

"It's been quite a night," the volunteer said. "The nurses have been popping down here one by one to update me. And to take a peek at my boyfriend. I suppose Wade filled you in that I'm dating Bruce Hunter."

"It came up," Adrienne conceded.

"He says his son has a key to his condo, which is fortunate, since I suspect Daryl and Reggie will beat us there," she went on. "See you in a few minutes."

"Absolutely."

While she was talking, Wade had driven down Safe Harbor Boulevard toward the harbor. As she hung up, they swung onto a drive that ran along the bluffs.

Adrienne's mind returned to an image of Reggie huddled at a closed garage, scared and shivering. "How do you suppose your father found him?"

"Dad asked me where I'd taken Reg, and I did mention his workplace." Admiration and regret mingled in Wade's words. "I didn't even think about checking there."

She wouldn't have, either. Clearly, Daryl had tuned into his grandson's mind-set. "I'm surprised your father doesn't want to take his grandson to see his own apartment."

"It's a mess."

"And he's embarrassed?"

"He wasn't too embarrassed to let me see it." Below, the harbor lay peaceful. "But I suppose this is different. First impressions and all that."

"I'm glad he's discovering his family." But what about the family Reggie longed for most? That was why he'd run away. Before they faced him, they'd better decide on a game plan, Adrienne thought. "Reg might get upset if you leave him with me tonight."

"Your house is his home, and he belongs with you as much as me," Wade replied. "I always carry an overnight bag in the trunk. Any reason I can't sleep over in your guest room?"

It was as near to a perfect solution as they were likely to hit on for tonight. "That would be wonderful."

"Done," he said.

They'd reached a large condo complex, Adrienne saw. She couldn't wait to hold her little boy.

LAUGHTER, HUGS AND the aroma of grilling hamburgers and onions—from a meal Renée was throwing together—transformed Bruce's condo into a warm gathering place. Wade was glad they were meeting here amid his grandmother's carved cabinets and other heirlooms.

He and Adrienne had arrived before his grandfather to find Daryl and Reg studying the photos in the dining room. "That's you?" the little boy had said incredulously. "Camouflage! Wow."

Daryl's weathered face had creased, close to tears, when he'd glanced up at the new arrivals. "Quite a kid, my grandson," he'd said.

The next half hour was a blur of embraces and stories as they shared their adventures. Wade and Adrienne also took the little boy into an alcove for a stern talk.

"You put yourself in danger tonight," Wade said.

"I'm sorry." He hung his head and then peeked up mischievously.

"This isn't a small thing, like forgetting a chore," Adrienne added sternly. "A lot of people were scared and upset. Don't ever, ever do anything like this again."

Reg's lower lip quivered. "I was only trying to find Dad."

"Part of growing up is considering the consequences before you act," Wade said. "And controlling your impulses. You really scared us. We love you so much."

"I love you, too," his boy said earnestly. "I promise I'll never run away again. And I keep my promises."

They both hugged him. "You think he'll remember?" Wade asked Adrienne after Reg rejoined his grandfather. "He was cold and scared out there, but I'm not sure that's enough of a punishment."

She thought it over. "After the holidays let's get him involved in volunteer work to pay back the community for all the trouble he caused."

"Good plan." Wade liked that idea. "What kind of stuff can a kid do?"

"Beach cleanup, for instance."

"Sounds like a good Saturday-morning activity. Or Saturday afternoon, if you're not too tired to join us."

"It would be fun."

As for Reg, his spirits quickly rallied as he ran from person to person, excited about being near his grandfather and great-grandfather, as well as Wade. He also returned frequently to Adrienne, touching her arm or hand before darting off again.

Her heart shone on her face as she tracked the little guy.

She was quieter than usual, careful around Wade, still unsure of him. And no wonder. He owed her a long talk… after he had a chance to frame what he meant to say. And to figure out what was holding him back.

When the six of them sat down around the long table, Wade realized he couldn't recall the last time the three generations of Hunter men—make that four generations—had dined together. "You came through tonight, Dad," he told Daryl.

Across the table, Bruce appeared on the verge of adding a sarcastic comment. However, his expression shifted quickly. "Yes, you did."

Renée handed around the plate of hamburgers. "From right to left, please. No collisions while we're passing."

"This smells great," announced Reg from between Wade and Adrienne. "Are you my grandma?"

"Shh." Bruce put his finger to his lips and then added in a stage whisper, "I'm working on it."

Renée cleared her throat.

"Hard," his grandfather said.

Wade didn't try to hide a grin. "Glad to hear it."

Bruce heaped a pile of fried onions on his plate. "You're a better detective than I gave you credit for, grandson. You figured out what was bothering my lady."

"Much as I appreciate the compliment, it was Renée who clued me in," he admitted.

"Well, I might have called the cops on you if you'd been as big a jerk as… Let's not finish that sentence," the older woman said tartly, and spritzed her burger with mustard. "You've got heart."

"I've got a heart, too," Bruce protested.

Her mouth twisted sardonically. "Rumor has it."

"Speaking of rumors, those folks at the hospital are the biggest bunch of snoops I ever met," he said. "Must have been a dozen of 'em trooped down to look me over."

Adrienne chuckled. "They're fond of Renée. And curious about the man in her life."

As they chatted, the food disappeared, followed by ice cream for dessert. Afterward, when Wade and Reg began clearing the table, Daryl joined them.

"Never thought I'd see him pitching in," Bruce muttered when his son was in the kitchen.

Renée poked him in the ribs. "Quit ragging on him. He's trying."

"Besides, he's the hero of the hour," Wade pointed out as he collected the condiments.

"He sure is." Adrienne had greeted Daryl with an embrace. He'd flushed, but it was obvious he enjoyed being admired for a change. Wade was glad she was meeting his family under such happy circumstances.

He watched appreciatively as she drifted into the living room, talking to Renée. Being friends would help the two women keep the men in line. Strong men needed strong women. Funny that he hadn't recognized that when he'd dated a loose cannon like Vicki.

In the kitchen Reg climbed onto a chair, and the three of them scraped, rinsed and loaded dinnerware into the dishwasher. Their teamwork fell into a natural rhythm.

Reg's patience wore out before they finished, though, and off he scampered. "Wish I had his energy," Daryl said.

Wade angled a glass into the top rack. "In case I haven't mentioned how grateful I am…"

"Don't make me out to be some saint, because you and I both know I'm not." Daryl gazed out the window onto Bruce's small dark patio. "I've been afraid to meet my own grandson, and I resented him, too."

"Resented him?"

"I was afraid you'd pick him over me." Daryl's hands clenched. "Before you two connected, I was your only family. Well, aside from the old man, but you guys weren't speaking."

Wade didn't bother to point out that families, like love, had no limits. "Today you more than made up for it."

Daryl's chest heaved. "Reg and I were looking at those old photos. Reminded me of the man I used to be. I can't be him again, but I can be a better one than I've become."

"No argument there."

"I'm not sure they hold AA meetings on Christmas Day," Daryl said. "But I'll search on the web."

Wade tilted his head in acknowledgment. Much as he'd like to help, this had to be his father's journey.

"By the way, I like that lady doctor of yours," Daryl went on.

"Me, too." So why was Wade having such a problem deciding what to say to her?

Right now he'd rather simply enjoy being here with this contentious but loving group. And especially with Adrienne and his son.


ON THE WAY home Wade swung by the hospital so Adrienne could pick up her car. Although they'd explained to Reggie that they'd all be staying at the house, he clung to her when she started to get out. Unsure how to respond, she glanced at Wade.

"Ride with your aunt," Wade told his son, to Adrienne's relief. "It's okay. You can trust us both to keep our word."

"Okay, Dad." Beaming, the little boy scrambled out of the cramped rear seat and took Adrienne's hand. "That was fun at Grandpa's house," he told her. "I mean, Great-Grandpa's."

"It was fun *after* we found you." Her breath clouded the chilly air. Thank goodness Reg wasn't still huddling in a doorway.

"I like both my grandpas."

"So do I." After all she'd heard from Wade, Adrienne had been apprehensive about meeting the men. Instead, she'd found them delightful company.

She hoped to be part of future celebrations, and not only as Reggie's aunt. But she had to be realistic.

Wade still hadn't commented about her disclosure. No doubt he was trying to be diplomatic, but his silence stung almost as much as a rejection.

By the time they reached her house, where Wade was waiting with his overnight bag slung over one shoulder, she felt as if she'd been gone for a week. And although it was only eight o'clock, the stress and excitement of the day had taken a toll.

"We'd better go to bed so Santa can visit," she told Reg when they were all inside.

Wade's eyebrow lifted at the mention of Santa. Perhaps he didn't believe in telling children fairy tales.

"He never brings me any of the cool new toys," the little boy complained.

Both Wade's eyebrows shot up.

"I told you, Santa has to save the expensive gifts for poor children." Adrienne unzipped her jacket and hung it in the hall closet. "So your family buys you the special things."

"Besides, you were naughty tonight," Wade pointed out. "If I were Santa, I'd leave a piece of coal in your stocking."

His son gave him a playful push. Wade caught the little boy easily, swung him around and hugged him while Reggie giggled.

"He does give me books," the little boy said when he was back on terra firma. "Those are special, too. When I'm bigger and Santa doesn't come here anymore, who'll give me books?"

"I will," Wade and Adrienne said in unison, and exchanged amused glances.

Reggie yawned.

"And so to bed," Adrienne concluded.

She meant to stay up after he was asleep so she and Wade could plan how to proceed over the next few days. Instead, her eyes refused to stay open. No sooner had she tucked in her nephew than Adrienne wandered down the hall as she'd often done during her residency after putting in a thirty-hour shift. She kicked off her shoes, fell across the bed with her clothes on and shut out the world.

IN THE DOORWAY, Wade debated whether to pull the covers over Adrienne. Since lifting and moving her would almost certainly wake her, he went to the hall linen closet, retrieved a comforter and spread that over her instead.

Downstairs he checked that the house was locked. In the den, the fake tree still glowed. The hall reminded Wade of Reg's birthday party. He'd barreled in here uninvited to be greeted by the scents of chocolate and cinnamon and by a longing for the kind of home he'd had as a child.

Memories clustered about him like wistful ghosts. Thanksgiving and their last-minute dinner... Sitting on that couch, showing Reggie how to pick out chords on the guitar... The wedding, when he'd sung with the children... So many memories. Most of all, that night he'd spent with Adrienne, when he'd felt surrounded by her love.

She did love him. She was afraid of it, though. She'd been afraid all along.

*So am I.*

Disturbed by his thoughts, Wade switched off the lights and went upstairs. In his room he took a photo from the shelf, a high school graduation photo of Vicki. At eighteen she'd twinkled with high spirits. A cute blonde, she wore her mortarboard at a rakish angle, with the tassel barely missing her eye.

For all her youthful gaiety, she'd been cruel to him. But she'd suffered, too. And now she lay in that cemetery while the world went on without her. Wade saw her as she'd been, vulnerable and unstable, a woman who, as her sister said, hadn't deserved to be born with a mental illness.

The last of his resentment faded. Though it was unintentional, Vicki had left him a precious gift with her death almost a year ago. His son. Make that two gifts: she'd also cleared the way for him to fall in love with Adrienne.

Time to bury the past, Wade thought. And to start working on the future.

## Chapter Nineteen

Adrienne awoke to the scent of orange-cranberry muffins
and the awareness that the two people dearest to her heart
were downstairs. For today, she intended to simply enjoy
being with them. Happiness was too precious to waste.

She showered and dressed in a silly red sweater embroi-
dered with a couple kittens in Santa hats. Vicki had given
it to her last year, and she prized it.

Downstairs in the kitchen, Wade wore an apron and a
patch of dough on one cheek as he removed the muffins
from the oven. At the crookedly set table, Reggie stuck a
butter knife in a tub of margarine.

"I'll bet you're hungry," Adrienne said.

Proudly, he pointed to the full coffeepot. "I made that.
Dad showed me how."

"You taught him to brew coffee?" It seemed to her like
a rather grown-up task.

After positioning the muffin tin on the stove, Wade set
down the pot holders. "When our son is determined to do
something, it's better to teach him the right way than let
him try on his own."

She conceded the point.

Reggie produced his tablet computer and, after a few
clicks, showed her a map of Safe Harbor's bus routes. "I'm
not s'posed to go out alone 'cause it's dangerous. But now
I can find my way if I have to."

Across the kitchen, Wade shot her a silent appeal. "Okay," Adrienne said. "Anytime you're tempted to do adult stuff, come to us first, okay?"

His head bobbed in agreement. "Can I pour you a cup?"

About to point out how heavy the carafe was, she caught herself. "Thanks for asking. Let your dad show you how."

With Wade's guidance and the aid of a pot holder, Reg filled her favorite mug. So what if he spilled almost as much as he poured? Thanks to Wade's instructions, it went into the sink.

As soon as the muffins were cool enough to eat, they dug in. The meal went fast, both because they were hungry and because Reg was impatient to open presents.

Santa had left *Presidential Pets* by Julia Moberg and a couple other picture books under the tree. Reggie flipped through them with interest and then set them aside for later. Next Wade insisted his son open Adrienne's packages. The little boy nearly got sidetracked by a computer puzzle game and had to be dissuaded from playing it immediately. He dived into another present, a hands-on science kit that Peter had recommended.

"We can both use this, okay, Dad?" he asked.

"You bet." Wade's smile seemed distracted.

*Don't think about what he might say later. Stay in the moment.*

Before tackling his remaining gifts, Reggie handed them each a small package, messily wrapped in Sunday comics. Opening hers, Adrienne removed a computer-printed booklet filled with photos Reg had shot during the year. There she was at Harper's wedding—an unflattering view from child height, but never mind that—plus there were pictures from school, sports camp and Mia's birthday party last summer.

"I love it." She hugged him.

Wade leafed carefully through his. "This is the best present anyone ever gave me."

Peering over his shoulder, Adrienne saw that Reg had taken shots not only of his father but also of the toy police station after they'd assembled it. And, as with Adrienne's book, he'd included an out-of-focus self-portrait with his little face scrunched and his tongue stuck out.

Priceless.

After gleefully accepting their thanks, Reg reached for a large package that bore Wade's name. "Can I open this next?"

"Of course," his father said.

It was a child-size guitar. Although small, it had a clear tone when Reggie ran his fingers across the strings.

"Now I can sing with you, Dad!" the boy exclaimed. "We can make a video."

"That's a great idea." Wade handed him a second gift, which turned out to contain an instructional DVD. "It'll take some work before we're good enough."

"Let's start now."

Adrienne hesitated. She wasn't ready for her men, as she thought of them, to go off on their own. "Wade and I haven't exchanged our presents yet."

Then she realized that only one package remained beneath the tree, the one she'd wrapped for Wade in the same paper she'd used for Reg's packages. A sparkly shape behind the tree was only a lump in the tree skirt, not a box.

Reggie noticed, too. "Where's Daddy's gift for you?"

Maybe Wade hadn't bought her anything, she thought, noticing a flush on the man's cheeks. "Grown-ups sometimes give each other the kind of gifts you can't wrap," she said. "Like dinner out."

"The truth is, I bought your aunt something too small to put under the tree." It was hard to tell whether he was joking. "How about you go play upstairs with that new game for a few minutes?"

"Why can't I see it?" his son demanded.

"You can, but she gets to see it first," Wade said. "In private."

Reg eyed him sternly. "I expect a full report."

"It's a deal."

Having struck a bargain, the little boy collected an armful of new possessions and hauled them away. That left Adrienne and Wade alone, sitting on the carpet.

They were overdue for a discussion about her inability to have children, yet in a rush of nervousness, she plucked the remaining package from beneath the tree. "I hope you like it."

He took it with a puzzled expression. "Thanks."

"It's okay if you forgot to buy me anything," she added.

"I didn't forget." With that cryptic remark, he slid off the ribbon and tore into the paper.

Hands clenched in her lap, Adrienne watched.

IT WAS A gorgeous sweater, soft, warm and an unusual shade of blue-gray. Adrienne had chosen this carefully. Pleased, Wade pulled it on, enjoying the warmth. "Thank you. Just what I need."

"Good." She sounded breathless.

Although last night he'd assumed he knew what to say, his whole body tensed. She'd already rejected him once.

Well, he wasn't about to let that scare him off. *Better get started.* Reaching into his pocket, Wade produced a black-velvet jeweler's box.

Adrienne sucked in her breath sharply. When he placed it in her palm, she let it sit there as if it might explode. Then, pressing her lips together, she pried it open.

A pair of gold earrings set with diamond chips caught the lamplight. "They're stunning."

*Hurry up before she thinks that's all there is.* "I'm hoping we can find a ring to go with those. The kind with a diamond."

After a silent moment that stretched far too long, she said, "You don't mind about not having children?"

Wade longed to reassure her, but he had to answer honestly. "Sure, I'm disappointed. I'd love to have kids with you."

Adrienne blinked, studying the earrings. "We could hire a surrogate."

"Either way, I want to marry you, if you'll have me," Wade said. "Funny thing—it's almost a relief that you won't have to go through a pregnancy."

"What do you mean?" Her startled gaze met his.

He reached out to touch her shoulder. "In my family relationships seem to be jinxed. Not only were the marriages unhappy, but my grandmother died after she fell down the stairs, and my mother died in a plane crash. I don't want any harm to come to you, and pregnancies, well, I understand they can get complicated."

"They're usually safe," she responded promptly. "That's really a concern for you?"

"Protecting you and Reggie is my number-one priority," Wade said fiercely. "Later we can talk about surrogacy or adoption, but that's not what matters most. You and Reggie mean everything to me."

Was she on the verge of tears? And if so, was that good or bad?

Adrienne swallowed. "I've always been the strong one, picking up the pieces for everyone else and protecting myself."

He squelched the impulse to argue. *Let her finish.*

"The thing is, I've discovered I'm stronger with you than on my own." A tear slid down her cheek.

"Then why are you crying?"

"I'm afraid to say yes."

"Why?" He kept hoping that he'd start to understand women—Adrienne, specifically—but he wasn't making much progress.

"I never expected to have my dreams come true." She ran her hands up his arms, along the soft sweater. "It's almost too much to ask. Like you said, our families are jinxed."

"How about I knock over a vase or something?" Wade joked. "To use up the bad luck."

They both laughed, and then Adrienne scooted across the carpet into his arms. "I guess nobody gets a guarantee."

"Only that we'll love each other as long as we both shall live." Wade had no doubts on that score.

They clung to each other, closeness deepening into a kiss. He'd have liked to carry her upstairs—well, being realistic, to lead her upstairs—and make love, but here came those racing footsteps.

In popped the cute little boy who'd brought them together. "Yay!" he shouted on seeing them cuddling. "You aren't fighting. Promise you never will, okay?"

"I'm sure we'll disagree occasionally," Wade said, adding for Adrienne's benefit, "Just keeping it real."

"I tend to be a little grumpy when I'm tired." Her words were muffled against his sweater.

"But we'll always fight fair, and we'll talk things out until we find a solution," Wade finished. "That's what husbands and wives do."

Reggie regarded them with rising excitement. "You guys are getting married?"

"Yes," Adrienne said.

"I've been waiting for that," Wade murmured against her hair.

"I thought I said it."

"Not till now."

"Can I walk you down the aisle, Aunt Addie?" Reggie asked.

"What about me?" Wade pretended to be hurt. "I was going to ask you to be my best man."

Reg drew himself up proudly. "I'll walk you both down the aisle."

What a brilliant idea. "Perfect," Adrienne said.

"That's our little boy." His heart swelling, Wade gathered them both into his arms.

His wife-to-be. His son.

His family.

\* \* \* \* \*

*Watch for more* SAFE HARBOR MEDICAL *stories
from Jacqueline Diamond!*